PURSUIT OF JUSTICE

OTHER BOOKS
BY WILLARD BOYD GARDNER:

Race Against Time

PURSUIT OF JUSTICE

a novel

WILLARD BOYD GARDNER

Covenant Communications, Inc.

Published by Covenant Communications, Inc.
American Fork, Utah

Printed in the United States of America
First Printing: January 2003

08 07 06 05 04 03   10 9 8 7 6 5 4 3 2 1

ISBN 1-59156-154-X

For my girls.

PROLOGUE

East of Parley's Canyon, Utah
Fall 1849

The funeral, like previous ones on the trail, was simple and brief. What might have constituted a rare tragedy in the Eastern United States, here was merely a footnote in a long list of heartrending incidents endured by the faithful Latter-day Saints making the arduous journey west into unknown territory. A wagon had slipped a wheel on a steep, makeshift road along a razor-sharp ridge leading across one of the last mountainous obstacles between the Saints and their valley home just several days away. The wagon and its three faithful passengers had fallen nearly a hundred feet, turning end over end through the sparse trees and huge boulders on the south side of the ridge. The sole survivor was only one year old—if that—and was now one of the many orphans destined to open the West under the parentage of any family willing to feed another hungry belly.

"Such a good and talented woman," said Anna McCray LeJeune, standing over two hastily dug graves.

"And a faithful husband and father, as well," said Anna's husband, Bartoleme LeJeune, a French-born Canadian who had joined the Church during the Missouri years. He pulled his trademark black canvas duster around his shoulders and said a brief prayer of his own to accompany the prayers already said on behalf of the deceased.

He put his arm around Anna and urged her from the graveside and back to the wagons to continue their trip. LeJeune had been the best friend of Anna's first husband, Lewis McCray, and had vowed to care for Anna after her husband's death from the ague. But LeJeune's relationship with Anna was not just a matter of responsibility and honor—it was the result of a deep and abiding love for this cultured and beautiful woman turned pioneer.

Loss was not a new experience for members of the LeJeune family. Anna, though still a relatively young woman, had already lost two brothers and a husband to the hardships of pioneer living. Despite these devastations and brutal persecution at the hands of those who wanted the Mormons gone, the LeJeune family was a strong, happy family, and Anna protectively and passionately nurtured her children, a handsome boy from her first husband and her two young girls with Bart.

And so it was that Anna held the orphaned baby boy wrapped in his only remaining possession—a colorful, ragged quilt. She looked at her husband, unable to find words for the question she wanted to ask him about the child. She need not have worried. A small nod from her good husband signaled the baby's acceptance into the LeJeune family, to be adopted formally once they reached the Salt Lake Valley and some semblance of civilization.

Anna looked wistfully over her shoulder at the wreckage of the wagon and its contents strewn on the rocks below.

"What of their possessions, Bart?" Anna whispered to her husband.

Even to ask such a question was to invite hostility from the rest of the train. Overloaded wagons contributed to many of the pioneers' hardships, and when someone insisted on bringing along any unnecessary items, others looked upon it as something akin to deliberate sabotage of the wagon train.

Bart looked at the orphaned boy in his worn clothing and ragged blanket. "We have what is most important, Anna. We can't carry more, can't ask it of the group. What food remained has been collected. That is all that matters."

"The box, Bart. What of the box? You know what it contains. You know what it meant to Rebecca and what it will someday mean to this boy and the Burns family." Anna toyed with a lock of the small boy's hair.

Bart simply shook his head. "I will not ask this group to wait while we fetch that box from the bottom of the canyon. They would not stand for it."

"But, Bart. The box . . ."

"These men," Bart said in a quiet voice, "their patience is worn, and they weary of trifles that slow the progress of the group. I cannot ask it of them. Life is full of hardships, Anna. The box is merely an obstacle to reaching the valley. It is not worth the life of one more soul."

"You'll return for the box? Please, promise me."

Bart looked at the worn faces of the men who'd pushed themselves beyond their limits day after day during the grueling trip west. These were the faces of men toughened by persecutions in the East and hardships in the West. They wouldn't stand for another delay, not when they were only days from the Salt Lake Valley and the chill of winter wasn't far off.

He turned his back on the wreckage and walked away.

CHAPTER 1

Park City, Utah
2002

I knew his face. I'd seen it a thousand times in my nightmares. He was the man who had murdered my best friend. I was propped on my side in the snow, adjusting my ski binding, when Raymond Hunt rode passively on the chairlift just ten feet above my head. He was wearing a two-toned silver ski jacket and a black stocking cap. His cold eyes scanned the hillside, but he didn't see me. The image that I'd nursed since the day Hunt killed Lewis and then disappeared was one of an emaciated criminal constantly on the run. The Raymond Hunt I was looking at now was a youthful, vigorous figure warmly bundled in an expensive ski parka and outfitted with trendy ski equipment; he was a man enjoying a vacation like any other normal person. But Raymond Hunt wasn't a normal person—he was an escaped convict and a merciless killer.

With my pulse racing, I looked down the mountain, then up. I had two choices. I could wait here at the midpoint and hope Hunt would come back down the mountain under the chairlift, where I'd pick him up again, or I could race for the lift line and hope to catch up with him at the top. I've never been good at waiting.

Snapping my boot into its binding and grabbing my poles, I turned my skis toward the lift line and took off downhill as fast as I could and still remain upright. Roughly six feet tall and a few soft pounds over a solid two hundred, I was a formidable force racing down the hillside. What I lacked in raw athletic ability I more than made up for in foolish courage as I sped on the edge of control down the mountain to the lift line, staying toward the edge of the run where the bumps were manageable at faster speeds.

Under each lift stanchion the snow had drifted to create large mounds that threw me high into the air. I was an accomplished skier and the runs at Park City were my home turf, so I took each jump in style.

I stopped once and looked over my shoulder to see both how far Hunt had ridden up the lift and to catch my breath. Hunt's black hat was edging over a crest in the hill and out of sight, so I turned back down the hill and raced on.

Several lift riders noticed my speed and the force with which I hit each mound under the lifts. Some whooped encouragement and others jeered when I hit the snowdrifts and lofted myself high in the air.

This time I won't lose him, I thought. *This time he won't have anywhere to run. This time, this time . . .*

By now I could see the lift line at the bottom of the hill and my thighs were screaming for more oxygen than my pounding heart could deliver. The result was a burning pain that I ignored. My legs would recover, but there might never be another chance at Hunt.

One last jump separated me from the head of the lift line. I hit it with enough speed to tuck my skis up and look down for a smooth place to land. The snow directly beneath me was smooth and well-groomed, and might have even made a great spot for a landing except for the length of orange plastic fencing that had been put up as part of the queue line at the trailhead. This was going to present a problem. The only good thing about my situation was that I was traveling far too fast through the air to make any real evasive maneuver, so all I could do was brace for the inevitable crash.

At first I could hear nothing but snow and vinyl rushing past my ears, but as my momentum slowed, I heard the crowd. Judging from their roar, my crash was magnificent. I heard all kinds of cheering and even received an Olympic freestyle score of 6.9 from a smarty-pants "judge."

I disregarded the multitude of small injuries I'd sustained in the wreck and clawed my way out of the orange fence, which clung to me like fish netting. Nearly every piece of ski equipment I owned was spread over the hill. My hat, a glove, sunglasses, skis, poles—everything not permanently attached to me had been thrown off in a different direction. It looked like the aftermath of a ski swap. I left what I didn't need and groped for my skis and one pole that was stuck in the snow close by.

With the pole hanging from my one gloved hand and both skis under my arm, I pushed my way to the head of the lift line.

"Owen Richards, Salt Lake City Police," I announced to the crowd. "I have to get to the top." I wouldn't have believed me either, but at the moment, I didn't care much about what anyone in the crowd thought. They could get as ugly as they wanted. "I'm a police officer. I have to get past," I said, pressing forward.

"Hey," said the lift operator as I barged in at the front of the line and waited for a seat to swing around. "You can't just cut in."

"Police officer. I don't have time to explain. I have to get to the top." A seat hit me in the back of the legs, and I swung aboard. "Official business," I offered over my shoulder as the lift swept me upward.

I looked for Hunt and tried to picture where on the hill he'd be by now. He was probably at the top. I did my best to fasten my skis back on without falling out of the chair, my eyes fixed on the slopes looking for Hunt. *I'll jump if I have to,* I thought.

My nose was running from the exertion, so I pulled my sleeve across my face. It left a long, crimson stain. The pain in my cheekbone was just beginning to register. I took a few deep breaths to get my wits about me, determined that a swollen eye and a nosebleed weren't going to slow me down.

"Hey, mister," I heard a voice say behind me.

I turned in my seat and saw two teenage snowboarding dudes sitting a couple of chairs back. One was waving my missing ski pole.

"Hey, thanks," I yelled back at them.

The boy holding my pole gave me a sneer, raised my pole above his head, and threw it to the ground like a javelin as hard as he could. "Don't cut in line, idiot!" he yelled.

I turned forward in my chair and tightened my grip on my remaining pole. I had no time for child's play. I turned back around to give the two boys a piece of my mind and noticed, in the chair directly behind me, the tortured look of a middle-aged woman and her young daughter. I presumed they didn't need to hear what I planned to say to the boys, so I took a cleansing breath and held my tongue. Besides, I'd already put on quite a show just getting to the lift. The teenage boys were still snickering to themselves. So what? At least they'd have a story to tell at school. I had a murderer to catch.

The scene on the slopes below was typical of any other day, yet strangely surreal. Near a trailhead, a woman was adjusting the straps on her husband's goggles, and farther down, an elderly man executed a shaky snowplow turn, sliding carefully from mogul to mogul. There were other people in colorful hats and bib overalls, talking and laughing, seemingly unaware of the vicious, subhuman killer-at-large among them.

As I neared the top of the lift, I realized how many directions Hunt could have gone and started to lose hope. I poised my skis to dismount from the chair, still looking for signs of Hunt and his dark ski hat. As my skis touched down on the ramp, I plunged my one remaining pole into the snow to give myself a good push and clear the lift. It snapped immediately, leaving me holding a useless piece of aluminum pipe with an ergonomic handle. I tumbled face-down onto the ice pack at the end of the lift. The two boys behind me weren't laughing anymore—they were howling.

"Hey, aren't you the guy who . . ." began the lift operator at the top.

I hurried to my feet, positioned my skis under me, and took off before I heard the end of his complaint. A few of the patrons on the lift behind me who hadn't had a chance to comment yet gave me their final thoughts (none of which were pleasant) as I pushed my way toward one of the runs.

Still holding tightly to the less-functional end of my ski pole, I struggled to gain control. I eventually made it to the edge of the most populated run and scanned the hill for Hunt's silver parka and black stocking cap. I could hardly believe it when I spotted his clothing. There he was, swooshing back and forth gently only several hundred feet away. A member of the ski patrol was heading my way who seemed quite anxious to talk to me.

"Follow me!" I yelled, pushing off down the hill.

Hunt didn't see me coming, and, by the look of his relaxed form, I was going to take him by complete surprise. The run was smooth, and I tucked what was left of my one pole under my arm, making a straight line toward his black cap.

The ski patrol was right behind me and had now multiplied into three people. They were yelling at me, but I couldn't have understood them even if I *had* been the slightest bit interested in what they were saying.

I'd lost my glasses in my fall at the bottom of the ski lift, so my eyes were watering badly from the wind. I wiped away what tears I could without throwing myself off balance. I was closing in on Hunt quickly and had attracted some attention. A couple of other skiers were now yelling at me to slow down. Instead, I dropped my piece of ski pole and prepared for Hunt. Seconds before impact, Hunt turned around to see what all the yelling was about and became the world's most opportune target. His eyes grew to fantastic dimensions, and his brow started to furrow at about the same time it became clear to him that I was deliberately going to bury my forehead in his sternum and that there was nothing he could do about it.

There was also nothing I could do about the fact that this man was not Raymond Hunt, and that he was probably going to be very upset after I crashed into him—if he was still conscious.

I contorted my body at the last second, trying to minimize the impact. Our bodies met with a sickening thud, and I could feel the air blow out of both of us. We tumbled together for about forty feet until momentum threw us apart and I slid another thirty on my own. The man in the silver coat came to rest up the hill from me, and I scrambled to reach him. He was shaking off the shock when he saw me coming, and then he cringed in fear.

* * *

A sincere apology and a detailed explanation of the situation smoothed things over with my victim.

"Hey, the way I look at it," he said, laughing, "I can tell all my friends in the San Fernando Valley that I was busted for murder on my ski vacation."

He was a middle-aged man who resembled Hunt only in that they shared a similar build and facial structure. How I could have mistaken the two was beyond me at the moment. The important thing was that I'd lucked out and pulverized a man with a healthy sense of humor.

It wasn't as easy to appease the lodge manager at the Park City Mountain Resort; he wasn't as friendly. It took a dump-truck load of groveling to put him at ease.

"Like I said, I'm a police officer with the Salt Lake City Police Department. I saw a man I recognized as Raymond Hunt, wanted for escape from prison and for the murder of a police officer."

"And this guy," said the lodge manager, a pear-shaped, pasty-faced man who looked as though he'd never even been on a ski slope, "Raymond Hunt—you say he killed your partner?"

"Yes," I repeated for the fourteenth time. "The guy escaped from the state pen and got trapped in an oil refinery near Salt Lake. He took a hostage and he ended up shooting one of our guys during the rescue. Then he . . ." I was beginning to get angry and emotional, having to go over this again and again for this buffoon, so I took a deep breath. ". . . he, Hunt got away."

"I talked to your shift supervisor at the department on the phone. He says that Raymond Hunt is dead."

"Presumed dead. He escaped down a wastewater culvert and they never found his body. Look, unless you want to press some kind of charge or something, I'm leaving. This is getting old fast." I started to get up from my chair and was pushed in the chest by the pear-shaped man's pointed finger.

"I don't want to see you on this mountain again. I've got a lot of important patrons, and I can't have some gung-ho rent-a-cop knocking people off the hill every day. If I see you back here . . ."

I calmly and deliberately removed the manager's finger from my chest and stepped past him. I shot him one last serious-police-business look and clunked out of his office in my ski boots, leaving him standing there with his mouth open, pointing his index finger.

I met Al outside the manager's office and walked right past him. I couldn't tell if his face showed signs of concern or if he was just holding back laughter.

"What in the wide world of sports is going on?" he asked, following me out of the building and onto the snowy streets of Park City. He ran his fingers through his sun-bleached blond hair. He was tall with an athletic, muscular build and naturally bronze skin. He had light hazel eyes and straight, white teeth that sparkled when he smiled. The female dispatchers at the department had given him the embarrassing nickname of "Mr. Delicious." Never, ever would he live that down.

Al was also one of my supervisors at the Salt Lake City Police Department. He was the SWAT team leader and got a little edgy when one of his team members flipped his lid.

"Look," I said, "I thought it was Hunt. That's all. I made a mistake."

"I guess you did. Come on, Owen, Raymond Hunt? Raymond Hunt is dead."

I stopped in my tracks and turned on him. "Presumed dead, Al."

"Okay," Al conceded, "presumed dead. I just want to make sure you're okay, that's all. I couldn't believe it when I saw you flying all over the place at the bottom of the lift. You looked like you'd just been shot out of a cannon. What kind of harebrained stunt was that?"

I took a deep breath and got ready to fire back at Al, but his lips started to curl into a smile, and I knew he was testing my sense of humor. Who was I kidding? I couldn't hold back a grin, and we both busted up.

"Did you catch my jump?" I asked. "That was some serious air. I should be competing, I'm telling you."

Al just shook his head.

We'd known each other for years, but we'd become very close after Raymond Hunt murdered my partner and lifelong friend Lewis McCray during a SWAT team hostage rescue. Al had been a shoulder to lean on, and I'd needed that. Raymond Hunt, presumed to have drowned in a wastewater culvert after the incident, still haunted my memories.

"I left the car over in the Park City Library parking lot. I hope it didn't get towed," said Al. "Let's get our stuff and head to my place for some grub."

Al's car was still in the lot when we got there. He drove a Subaru wagon that had seen many a ski on its Yakima ski racks. The car next to us had parked so close that I couldn't get the passenger-side door open.

"Hey, buddy," I said to the car's invisible owner as if he were standing there, "any closer and I'd need a can opener to get in."

"Park a little close, did he?" said Al. He never got too fired up about things. "I'll pull out so you can squeeze in."

"What kind of car is that, anyway?" I looked closer at the little sedan. "I haven't seen a Chrysler K-car in years."

Al looked over my shoulder at the plain brown car with its square fenders and boxy interior. "Chrysler had its moments," he said as we drove away, "but the K-car wasn't one of them."

Al had a Mahogany Hills address not far from Kimball Junction, and he never heard the end of it from his friends who couldn't even afford to eat up in the trendy Park City area, let alone live there. Al always countered by claiming that he was merely house-sitting for some long-lost relative. None of us knew for sure.

Al's house was a palace by my standards, but the lodge-style mansion fit right in with the Snyderville neighborhood where all the streets were named after famous skiers. The outside of the home was stucco and massive logs, with sheets of tinted glass that promised a spectacular view of the peaks and the ski resorts. Although the valley was heavily developed, you could still see some open meadowland nestled between subdivisions.

"So, do you still like the view?" I asked as we drove, pointing to a strip of half-built condos dug into the hillside at the bottom of Al's neighborhood.

"We're having a minor boom," Al said.

"I hear people are coming from all over looking for houses. What's with the house for sale across the street from your place? I thought everything worth having in Park City was pretty much snatched up."

"That's what everyone thinks. That house has been empty for months. The kid next door takes care of it."

"Maybe I should buy it," I said.

"You got a cool million in your pocket?" asked Al.

"You're kidding!"

"Nope."

Al fished in his pocket and pulled out the world's smallest cell phone.

"I invited Amanda up for dinner," he said as he dialed.

"Good work, Batman. You've been seeing a lot of her lately. Want me to make myself scarce?"

"No," Al said. "I don't. Now be quiet. Oh, hi Amanda . . . no, not you, I was talking to Owen." Al's voice rose one lovesick octave, and he forgot all about me while he and Amanda exchanged sweet nothings. I made gagging gestures and basically acted like a teenager until he eventually hung up and stuffed his cell phone back into his pocket.

"You two don't want to be alone?" I asked as we drove into Al's garage.

"No, she's expecting you to be here."

"You don't know the first thing about dating, do you?"

"Tell me all about it, O Great One." Al rolled his eyes and got out of the car.

"Well, first, you don't ask your buddy to hang out on dates with you. And, second, if I had a girlfriend like that, I'd be married by now."

"What are you talking about? Aren't you the same guy who's stringing along Lewis's cousin, that redheaded girl from Missouri?"

"Hey, look," I said, taking my skis from the rack on top of the car, "if Julianna McCray were on her way to my mountain hideaway, I wouldn't have you hanging around to spoil the mood, friend or not."

"Well, lover boy," Al said, "how is it going between you two? Do you think you have a chance with her?"

"I think I have a shot," I said. "A long shot."

"Maybe you should invite her to your next skiing exhibition. Your display of talent today pretty much makes the Olympics seem amateurish."

"Funny."

We shuttled all of our ski stuff to a closet in the garage and went inside.

The inside of Al's place was as spectacular as the outside and could have been a Parade of Homes feature attraction.

The décor had probably been done by one of the swanky interior design places downtown. I could tell because the less-lived-in areas looked completely nonfunctional. Right in the middle of the formal dining room table was a gigantic arrangement of fake fruit and flowers that left no room for plates. A life-size stone carving of a dog on its haunches sat near the main entry. Then again, maybe it wasn't as nonfunctional as I thought—it looked like a great place to hang a hat and jacket.

While Al dumped his wet ski sweater in the laundry room, I examined a new picture that hung in a carved wooden frame in the family room.

"I haven't seen this before," I said. "Must be an expensive piece."

"What, Robert Duncan?" Al stuck his head out of the laundry room to see which painting I was looking at. "Isn't that great? I didn't realize you knew art." Al seemed surprised.

"Actually, I'm quite the expert. If it doesn't look like it came rolled up in cellophane I figure it must be fine art. I can see the brush strokes on this one, so it must be really expensive fine art."

Al shook his head and went back into the laundry room. "Brush strokes," he mumbled.

"Are you sure you want me to stay?" I asked again.

"Yes, you haven't seen Amanda for a while." Al emerged from the laundry room. "We're just going to eat some dinner and relax. And you, my friend, aren't going anywhere."

"Wait a minute—wait just a minute. Amanda isn't bringing a lonely friend or someone, is she?"

Al laughed. "Hey, that's a good idea. I'm sure she can arrange it. Do you want me to call her back?" Al reached for his phone again.

"Don't touch that phone. You know better than that, anyway. There's only one woman for me—that beautiful redhead from Kansas City." Just thinking about her made me feel like singing. It was easy to act that way when the girl of your dreams was just that—a dream. If I thought I had a real chance with her, I might have acted a little more dignified.

"You're not going to break into song, are you?" asked Al.

"Do you want me to?"

"Do you want another black eye?" Al threw his keys at me and disappeared into the bathroom.

"Do I really have a black eye?" I mumbled to myself, touching my cheek gently.

I glanced at myself in the front hall mirror and rubbed my cheek. Yep. It was starting to color already.

I plopped down on the plush sectional sofa and curled my toes into Al's carpet. The radiant floor heat made the large room feel warm and inviting.

"Okay, I'll stay," I yelled into the other room. "But I'm just here for the entertainment and the free food." I peeled off my outer wool sweater and focused on Al's sixty-inch TV. Picking up the remote and turning it over in my hand, I just shook my head. There were too many buttons for me to figure out.

"Does this thing come with a book for dummies?" I asked, tossing it to Al as he walked back into the room. "Get me some baseball, Jeeves."

"It's February," Al said, pointing the device at the big screen and selecting a program about the dangers of winter weather. Some super-survival nerd was reposed on a bed of pine boughs in front of a fire that he no doubt built by rubbing sticks together. He warned Al and me not to sleep on the cold ground or we'd lose body heat through transfer with the earth.

"Borrring. Get me something else."

While Al channel-surfed, I put my feet up on the oversized ottoman and made myself even more comfortable. Al found a rebroadcast of a Jazz game and threw the remote in my lap. He went into the kitchen where he could see the television over the back of the couch, donned an apron, and started preparing dinner.

The game was nearly over, and after the last shot rolled around the rim and threatened to steal a win from the Jazz, I got up and wandered over to the window seat to look at the city lights twinkling in the darkness.

"Are you sure you're okay?" Al asked.

"About what?" I answered.

"About today. I know you and Lewis were pretty close friends. More like brothers, probably. Losing Lewis was hard on all of us—most of all you."

"Are you asking if I've blown a head gasket?"

"No, but you know people."

"Are you suggesting that the department is going to question what happened on the hill today?"

"They might. Everyone's pretty tense right now with the Olympics and everything."

I knew I was currently in the running for a position with the detectives, but I could suddenly see that swirling down the drain. "What are they going to do to me, make me work nights and weekends?" I joked.

"Or worse," Al said in a serious tone.

After the shooting at the refinery, I'd been assigned a compulsory psychological evaluation along with everyone else involved in the incident. What was supposed to be a two-week debriefing turned into a two-month ordeal because I told the department psychologist that shortly after Lewis's death I'd participated in the Mormon War of 1838. The story went over swell. The result was an embarrassing two more months on the couch with the department shrink. Most of the guys knew I was spending a lot more time with the psychologist than was normal, but none of them said anything. As far as I knew, the record of my temporary bout with insanity and the subsequent therapy sessions were sealed in my psychological file. The only document open to supervisory review was a summary of my suitability to return to work that thankfully didn't mention the phrase "grief-induced delusions," which had come up several times before and during my sessions.

I didn't really know what to say to Al. I knew he was right—the department wasn't going to overlook today's little Hunt episode in light of what they did know about my fanciful past. As the SWAT team leader, Al had been made aware of my suspected mental instability, but trusted that it was over and done with. He probably didn't know any of the details. I'd hoped all that was behind me, but I suppose people never really forget.

"I could always retire and become a monk," I said. "What do you think a monk makes? You know, like in a month?"

Al rolled his eyes.

"Before taxes," I said as he shook his head.

The phone rang and Al answered. He said hello and then shot me a glance. I knew he was talking about me. He turned his head and retreated into the dining room down the hall so I couldn't eavesdrop. All I could do was look at the television and ignore the commercials that had taken over the set.

After several minutes, Al came back into the living room. "That was Lieutenant Michaels," he said.

I didn't say anything.

"He wants me to take you off the SWAT call-out list for a while. They'll talk to you about it when you go back to work. They called a supervisors meeting to discuss the issue."

I clenched my jaw and took a deep breath, staring at the television. That fired me up inside, but I wasn't going to allow myself to blow in front of Al. He was one of my last real friends.

"News travels pretty fast," I said, as soon as I could with some kind of control.

"I'm sorry, man," Al said. "I can't believe they're taking it this far. It wasn't that big of a deal." He put the phone down and busied himself with dinner. "Don't worry buddy, I'm going to be at the meeting. I got your back covered."

That was Al. He had the uncanny ability to sense a need and come running to help out. I liked working on his shift. He was always there to back you up.

It took a few minutes to compose myself. The whole situation was making me a little emotional, and I needed to sort things out. I wanted to talk about it, but I was reluctant, so I started setting the table instead. Dinner preparation was well under way, and the smell of roasted chicken filled the room.

"I guess you'd better hear it from me first," I said, putting a fork down alongside a large stoneware plate.

"Hear what?"

"The reason the department is treating this the way they are," I said.

"Do I need to sit down?" asked Al.

"It might not hurt."

CHAPTER 2

Al stopped tossing a salad and set his bamboo utensils down on the marble island in the kitchen.

"After Lewis's death," I said as I wandered into the kitchen, "you know, when I took Julianna back to Kansas City after the funeral?"

"Yeah."

"I had . . . an experience."

"What do you mean, 'an experience'?" Al moved a mixing bowl out of his way and leaned against the island.

"Like a short departure from the realm of the sane."

Al was looking concerned now and pulled a kitchen stool out from the bar and sat down. He hadn't been privy to any of the details of my psychological profile, and I hadn't shared any of this with anyone other than the department psychologist.

"I took a little trip 'round the bend, so to speak," I said. I was having a hard time finding the right words. I was taking a chance telling Al any of this, but I had a suspicion that he'd know about all of it soon enough anyway. I knew that "sealing a file" was a loose concept in any government agency. My file was probably flapping wide open by now.

"'Round the bend?" Al didn't understand.

"Julianna took me to a place outside of Kansas City. It was beautiful country. Anyway, I was taking a picture of her, and then suddenly it happened."

"What happened?"

"I don't exactly know what happened. I just . . . lost it."

"What do you mean, you lost it? You were taking a picture and then what? Did you say something to Julianna?"

"No, I was taking a picture of Julianna standing in the trees by this creek. Then suddenly, she wasn't there. I mean, there was someone there, but . . ."

Al shifted on his stool and leaned in a little closer.

I wasn't making much sense, so I collected my thoughts before I went on. "There was a different woman there, and she told me that her brother was in trouble. I heard some gunfire, and then she led me to this boy who was getting stomped into next week by three of the most vile Missouri pukes I've ever seen. And they all had rifles. I'm not kidding, Al, it was as real as you and me right now."

Al shifted again on his seat and leaned back, folding his arms, apparently not overly comfortable with my story.

"These guys were really beating this kid, so I fired a couple of rounds into a tree to scare them away and took the boy to a small settlement, kind of like a little log village with oxen and wagons and stuff. Nothing modern. I just figured I was lost in the Missouri hillbilly country. After that, I couldn't find anything. No road, no phone, nothing."

"So, you didn't know where you were?" asked Al.

"No idea. I did find my truck, but these Missouri guys were really mad at me. They chased me through half the county. I ended up in a place that everyone was calling Far West."

"Far West?" Al looked confused.

"Yeah, Far West, but the weird thing is, I had just been to Far West with Julianna, and it had been a historical sight, with a plaque and everything. But it wasn't a town—just a historical site in a field. This Far West wasn't that Far West. I mean, this one had cabins and stores and people. It was like a real little western town."

"Sounds like a bad dream," Al said.

I pulled out a stool and sat down next to Al at the end of the bar. "I met this guy, Bart LeJeune. He was kind of like a lieutenant in the army there. He was in charge of the Mormon spies who were tracking enemy mob movements, and . . ."

"Wait a minute. So, were these real people, or were you imagining this?"

"It was real, Al. As real as . . . It was real. At least it felt real. I don't know, just listen."

Al nodded.

"This LeJeune guy was really suspicious of me. He had me followed and everything. The Mormons at Far West were getting ready for a heavy siege, so they didn't trust anyone. At first I didn't like LeJeune, but . . . after a while we became friends."

I scooted the fruit bowl out of the way so I could have more room for my arms on the counter. I was anxious to tell the whole story because, even when I'd told the psychologist, I had left out a lot—especially when it became apparent that the psychologist was mentally fitting me for a straitjacket and a padded room.

"So, anyway, I left the little town and no sooner had I gotten out of there than I got captured."

"Captured?" said Al.

"Yes, captured. Some guy they called Bogart. Mean as . . . well, he was really mean. They blindfolded me and beat me within an inch of my life. I'm serious Al, I thought I was really going to die."

"What was Julianna doing all this time?"

"That's just it—she wasn't there. I thought I'd lost her. By this time, it had been several days and I was going out of my mind about her."

"Out of your mind, huh?"

I gave Al a well-earned stern look. "Yes, funny man. I was tied, gagged, and near death when the Mormons came and hosed the place. There was a battle, and people were shooting, and . . ." There was a lot more I wanted to tell Al, but the details would have to wait. "Anyway, these Mormons came and blasted the place. They rescued some of their own prisoners, and then they all left. Meanwhile, I hid in the rushes along a river. Eventually, everyone just left the area. I think they'd had enough for one day.

"I met up with the kid who was getting beat up, Elias, the brother of the woman in the beginning. He helped me get back to Far West."

"The kid who was getting beat up helped you get back to Far West?" Al was trying to follow along, but the story was getting a little convoluted.

"Yeah, exactly. We got back to Far West, and I was just about dead. I'm not exaggerating, Al, I was just about gone. I was spitting up blood and gore, and—"

"I get the picture," said Al.

"A couple of strangers prayed over me, and after a day or two I felt a lot better. Then Elias left the city to fetch his sister and got captured, just like I had. He was trying to get back to the village, um, the little mill town, called . . ." The name slipped my memory momentarily.

Al interjected. "Was it called Haun's Mill?"

"Yes, that's it." I slapped the counter. "Jacob Haun's mill."

"Wait." Al put his hand up to interrupt me. "So far, you've been to Far West during the siege and to Crooked River during the battle. It makes perfect sense that you are now going to Haun's Mill. Go ahead. I know what comes next. You have my undivided attention."

"I'm serious about this Al. I only said a few things about this to the psychologist after Lewis died, and he really got worked up about it. I nearly lost my job. They must still think I'm crazy. I'm not."

"I know you're not crazy, Owen, but this is pretty heavy stuff."

"It was so real to me, Al, as real as . . . I don't know if I was physically at those places, but I do know that something very real and significant happened to me. I know it was real. Call me crazy, but . . ."

"I'm sorry, Owen." Something in Al's countenance softened.

"I know how nutso this sounds, Al. But something happened. It changed my mind about a lot of things."

Al nodded and went to the oven to check on the roasting chicken. "So, how did this all end?" he asked, standing at the stove.

"Elias had gone after his sister, Anna, who looks exactly like Julianna. She was at the mill, and Elias went to bring her back to Far West. It was safer in Far West. But the mobs caught him.

"LeJeune and I went to rescue him. And then, we had to go to . . . the mill." I had to stop talking. Of all the things I remembered about Missouri, the mill was the most vivid. It was pure carnage, like nothing I'd ever seen. It was beyond description. "Al, the mill was under attack when we got there. You can't imagine."

"I can, Owen. I'm familiar with the Haun's Mill massacre."

"It was . . ." I rubbed my hands over my eyes, trying to block out the memory.

"The woman who looked like Julianna," I said, "she was gone. A small group of mobbers had taken her and another girl as hostages, and so we followed them—tracked them, actually. When we found them, we got them back. Bart LeJeune, me, and Elias—Anna McCray's brother—we . . ."

"Wait a minute, wait. McCray? Don't you think it's a little much that Anna's last name is the same as Lewis's?"

"Yes, Al, but it's not what you think. This isn't just me having some weird delusion over Lewis McCray's death. It all makes sense in the end, just listen.

"Anyway, the rescue, it was . . . You should have seen Bart LeJeune trying to use my rifle. He didn't even know how to look through the scope . . . That's not important though. Anna, the woman who looked like Julianna, was pregnant—really pregnant. After the rescue, we went as far as we could toward Far West, but Anna wasn't going to make it. The baby was breach, and she just wasn't doing well." I stopped to think about how I would tell Al the rest of the story. Al and I didn't talk about religion very much.

I took a deep breath. "What happened next . . . I don't exactly know what you'll think of this, but . . . I prayed for a miracle."

Al didn't have the shocked reaction I was expecting. He seemed to accept what I was saying without hesitation. "You prayed for a miracle, and . . ."

"You have to understand. I'm not, well, I wasn't a praying person. I felt like I should have been able to help Anna, but I was helpless. Even when they beat me at Crooked River, I didn't feel that helpless." I took another breath and tried to fight back tears. I didn't want to let Al see me cry. I had no idea what his reaction was going to be.

"This thing was so real," I said once I'd gained my composure. "There was no other solution but to pray. I'd never been very good at praying. But I felt something. It was the same kind of something that I'd felt at Lewis's funeral. It was the same feeling. There was no mistaking it."

Al was nodding, looking at me through a serious set of eyes, and I could see that he understood.

"When I got back to the group, the baby had been born. Anna was fine. It was a miracle. I know it was a miracle."

Neither of us spoke for a few moments.

Al finally said, "So, what happened then?"

"Nothing. That was it. Then it was over. Before all this started I'd been standing there taking a picture of Julianna McCray. Then I lived about two weeks in la-la land, and then I was standing there with Julianna again. She was just talking to me like nothing had happened. I will never forget what I felt during that small moment of time. I think I had every emotion known to man."

"Wow," Al said. "That's a pretty amazing story."

"Not only that, but those people really existed. I haven't ever said anything to Julianna, but when she told me about her family history . . . I recognized the people immediately. She told me the story about the breach birth and everything. I knew every detail and then some. The baby that Anna had was Julianna's great-great-something grandfather . . . so he was also Lewis's ancestor. They named the baby Lewis McCray, after his father. Lewis Owen McCray."

Al shook his head and exhaled. "And all that took place in a matter of seconds?"

"Yes, less than seconds."

"And that's why you had to keep going to counseling after the rest of us were done?"

I nodded, got up, and walked to the sink. "I didn't go into any detail with the psychologist. When I started to say something about it, his eyes lit up and I knew I'd made a big mistake. It's just that I felt like the whole experience had really set things straight for me. I wasn't worried about Lewis's death anymore. I felt really . . . comfortable about it."

"And now this."

"Exactly," I said. "Now this. I'm telling you Al. I'm not all goofed up about Lewis's death. I just thought I saw Raymond Hunt today. That's the truth," I finished, looking straight into Al's eyes.

"I recognize when someone is telling the truth, Owen."

Neither of us spoke for a few minutes. Al checked dinner again and put a few more dishes on the table.

I was trying to gauge what kind of effect my story had on Al. So far, he'd responded better than I'd expected, but I could tell he was still trying to take it all in.

"It's almost like the life we see around us isn't all there is," I finally said. "Like there's a higher purpose to all this."

Al didn't speak for a few moments. Then he said, "Yeah, it's almost like that, huh?"

I was visited by a peaceful, calming feeling that I'd experienced before, once at Lewis's funeral and then again during my experience in Missouri. And, to a lesser degree, I'd felt that soft warmth several times since then. After I'd been to Missouri with Julianna to visit her family, I started to read a paperback copy of the Book of Mormon given to me by Lewis years earlier. I had made it a habit to read several passages each night before I settled into bed, and what had started as merely a tribute to Lewis's memory soon became a comforting ritual.

It was difficult reading the archaic phrases and obscure symbolism, and much of it passed before my eyes without my mind comprehending anything. But there were passages that caught my attention, either because they felt strangely familiar or because they provoked significant questions. I carefully marked each scripture and then dog-eared those pages. When more pages were folded over than were not, I knew I had to do something. After several sessions with the missionaries, I held in my heart a simple yet undeniable testimony of the purpose of life and the role of the Savior.

I needed to talk to someone who would listen and even believe in me, but at this point I'd already dropped a big enough bomb on Al with my Missouri tall tales. Besides, I didn't feel like a group hug, so I walked slowly behind Al's back to the sink and picked up a dish towel. I twirled it up and snapped Al right between the shoulder blades.

"But," I yelled, lunging out of the way of a lightning-fast stroke with a bamboo salad fork, "I say one little thing about this to a psychologist and suddenly he's treating me like the keynote speaker at an alien-abduction survivor reunion." I ducked behind the kitchen island.

"I always wondered where they found keynote speakers for those things," said Al, leaning around the island and rapping me on the head with the fork.

I blinked away a few shooting stars. "Oh, you slime bucket."

* * *

Amanda was Al's new girlfriend. They'd met under the worst circumstances—at the refinery where Lewis was killed. She was the process engineer called in to give our officers information about the refinery after Hunt took a girl hostage on their compound. Al, as the SWAT team leader, had worked closely with Amanda, and their relationship had taken off from there.

I hadn't seen much of Amanda since the incident, but I'd heard a lot about her from Al. He really liked her, and they had dated quietly until recently, when things seemed to be getting more serious.

Amanda arrived at Al's place just in time to eat. She was average height—not the tall, lanky model type—but had a muscular, athletic build. She was strikingly beautiful—her mink-colored hair nearly outshone her glistening brown eyes.

"Owen, I'm so glad to see you here," she said when she arrived at Al's front door. She had a basket bundled with a red-checkered cloth and a large plastic pitcher full of lemonade.

"Here, let me take that from you," I said, lifting the basket from her and peeking under the cloth. The aroma that wafted from the basket smelled like my Aunt Etta's kitchen. Etta wasn't really my aunt—she was Julianna's aunt—and her kitchen always smelled like something baking. I'd grown to like that about her.

"The rolls were hot when I left," Amanda said as she set down the lemonade and unveiled the glazed goodies. "They're barely warm now. Traffic up the hill was terrible. A guy in a silver BMW just about knocked me off the road. I had to jerk out of his way, hit the gas, and blow by him on the shoulder."

"Whoa. Hot Rod Mama," I said.

"Yeah, I was pretty embarrassed when I saw the moose he'd swerved to avoid."

"Wow, a moose, huh? I'm sure glad your rolls survived the trip," I joked.

"They'll be great," Al said, taking Amanda's coat. "I'm just glad you arrived safely."

"You look so domestic in your apron, dear," Amanda told Al. She hooked her finger on the front of the apron and pulled him to her. She gave him a soft kiss on the lips, made awkward because I was watching. Al was quite shy about such things, but Amanda didn't seem to mind.

"Oh, Owen, what happened to your face?" Amanda asked.

"A little spill on the ski hill today," I said, turning to Al, who was just opening his mouth to say something. I gave him the old zip-the-lips signal and a serious glare. He coughed back a laugh but didn't say anything.

"Looks like you're going to have a shiner there." Amanda reached up to touch my cheek.

"It's nothing a few days won't cure," I said.

Amanda took the rolls from me and went into the kitchen to set them on the table. Appropriate for the indoor picnic we were having, Amanda was wearing faded Levi 501s and a red V-neck sweater. The kicker, in my opinion, were her shoes. She was wearing original Asics Tigers—red, white, and blue—the sneaker of champions. She and Al went well together.

We set the table with roasted chicken, baked broccoli and rice casserole, green salad, homemade rolls, and fresh-squeezed lemonade. Al said a prayer, and then I loaded my plate.

Al and Amanda exchanged pleasantries and lovey-dovey glances all through the meal. I almost threw up. When Al started clearing the dishes, Amanda finally asked me the inevitable question.

"So, I hear you and the banker lady aren't a couple anymore," she said, referring to my old girlfriend.

I gave Al my best you're-a-big-mouth look. He just grimaced and shrugged, as if Amanda had tortured him for the information and he'd had no choice but to crack.

"Al tells me about all your romantic adventures, Owen," she said.

"Romantic adventures?" I scoffed. "My love life reads more like a P. G. Wodehouse short story."

"Oh, I can't believe that," Amanda said, raising her eyebrows. "Although, you do look a little like Bertie Wooster."

"Where in the world did you find this woman, Al?"

Al shrugged and gave me a smug smile.

"Anyway, it's true," I said. "Didi and I didn't see eye to eye."

"And why was that?" Amanda winked at Al.

"Why do I get the feeling that you already know all of this?" I asked.

"I just want to hear it straight from the horse's mouth. That way it's not gossip," Amanda said.

I sighed and shook my head.

"Come on, fess up," Al said.

"Yes, Owen, fess up." Amanda lifted a crystal cover off a cake that looked like it had been baked by some world-famous pastry chef.

"This looks exquisite," said Amanda.

I whispered to Al, "Fudgy chocolate layer cake from Dan's Grocery?"

"Shh, I want her to think I baked it," he whispered. "Why do you think I was wearing an apron?"

"Hey, you guys, quit whispering like schoolgirls. Besides, I saw the cake box in the trash compactor. Nice try, Al. Now, back to the juicy details. What of the blond, rich babe?"

"It all came to an abrupt halt several weeks ago—it wasn't pretty. We just weren't meant for each other."

"Oh, come on, Owen," Al said, "tell her everything. You aren't going to get away with the short version."

"All right, if you must know . . ."

"Oh, we must," said Amanda.

"I bumped into her while on a date."

Amanda gasped. "You or her?"

I smiled. "Her. She was out with one of the guys at the bank. You should have seen the look on her face."

"How did you 'bump' into her, Owen?"

"Well, I was working—in uniform—and I was dispatched to a motorist assist. It seems that Mr. Banker—I don't know his name—locked the keys in Didi's Jaguar during their little date."

"No!" said Amanda.

"Yes. It gets better. The whole time, Deirdra was trying to pretend she didn't know me, and he was trying to pretend that the Jaguar was his."

"And . . ." said Al. He couldn't wait for me to get to the punch line.

"And," I said, "after I'd gotten the door unlocked and Mr. Banker had made a few disparaging comments to me about my profession—"

"This is great," said Al. "You won't believe this, Amanda. This is the stuff legends are made of."

"Actually, I did steal a line from my favorite Richard Sharpe movie. When it was all over, I walked up to Didi, trying to keep from busting a gut, grabbed her by the shoulders, and said in my best British accent, 'It's a dark night out. You should've brought a man with you.' She was so shocked that she couldn't even speak. Mr. Banker just about hyperventilated. Then I handed Didi her keys and said, 'I'll see you later, much later, sweetheart,' and I drove off in my patrol car."

"Oh no—you didn't!" said Amanda, putting her hand over her mouth.

"Oh yes he did," said Al.

I just nodded, a big smile growing on my face. "I haven't heard from her since. I now conduct all my banking business at Mr. Banker's branch. Oh, he loves me. I'm thinking of buying a house so he can process the loan."

"I know you better than that. So, you and Didi are no more." Amanda was now filling glasses with milk.

"She's history."

"That sets the stage for the good-looking redhead from Missouri," Amanda said. "Lewis's beautiful cousin."

"What?" I said to Al. "Am I your only source of entertaining gossip?"

"I take what I can get, bro."

"I want to hear all about her," said Amanda.

"All I can say is, she is hot."

"Oh, really?"

"She's tall, about five-eight or nine, slender but athletic. And her figure is . . ."

"Owen?" Al raised an eyebrow.

"She's gorgeous," I said to Amanda.

"Just your type, then? Tell me, is there anything about her personality that you've noticed yet, or is this relationship sort of a 'Didi' thing?"

"She's nothing like Didi," I said.

"She's gorgeous and talented," said Al. "She and Owen are kind of like the odd couple."

"Oh, thank you, *Mr. Delicious.*" I said to Al. Then I turned to Amanda. "She's also very nice. A little too nice, in fact."

"I think he digs her," Amanda said to Al.

"We have a couple of obstacles to work through," I continued.

"Like she lives halfway across the country?" said Amanda. "That can't be very conducive to a budding relationship."

"Yeah," said Al, "and something about religion."

Amanda was just as thoroughly Mormon as Al was, so they both understood the implications of me dating a nice Mormon girl.

"There is one easy solution to this problem, you know," said Amanda.

"Maybe," I said. "I'm just not sure Mormonism is ready for me yet."

"Yeah," said Al, laughing, "Moroni would drop his trumpet if you got baptized."

"Look who's talking," I changed the subject, "the geriatric dating couple. Moroni would eat his trumpet if you got married. Besides, isn't being single at your age against your religion or something?"

Amanda beamed a huge thank-you smile at me and turned an accusing eye on Al. "You heard him, Mr. Delicious. What do you have to say to that?"

"What? Did you pay him or something?" Al asked Amanda.

Amanda smiled. "No, Owen is just more astute than you are."

"Jerk," Al said to me.

"Nitwit," I answered.

The soothing sound of the multitone doorbell prevented a full-scale brawl in the kitchen. Amanda went to the door while Al and I threw a few more insults at each other and stuffed fudgy chocolate into our mouths.

After Amanda left the room, Al put up his hands in surrender. "Seriously, Owen," he said, "I'm going to have to say something about your adventure on the mountain at tomorrow's meeting."

"Yeah, I just made a mistake. I can handle the fallout."

"But everything we talked about—that stays with me."

"I'd appreciate that."

"No problem, man. I got you covered." Al stuffed another forkful of cake into his mouth.

"Besides, can it get much worse than this?" I said, licking the chocolate ring around my lips.

"I can't see how." Al sighed.

Amanda returned from the entryway wearing an expression of disbelief.

"What's the matter? Who is it?" asked Al.

"It's not for you." She turned to me. "It's for you, Owen. It's the FBI."

CHAPTER 3

I'd worked with special agents from the FBI before. For the most part they were just regular cops. But it was unsettling to have them drop by for a visit, especially after what happened to me earlier that day.

Two men dressed in slacks, white shirts, and ties greeted me at Al's front door. They looked just like missionaries except for their Marker winter jackets, no doubt purchased for them by Uncle Sam for special duty in Park City during the Olympics.

"I'm Owen Richards," I said to the one who stood directly in the doorway. He was probably about five-foot-ten with dark, wavy hair. His face was clean shaven, but a heavy five o'clock shadow suggested he'd had a long day.

"Mr. Richards," he said in a heavy New York accent, like a Brooklyn street tough. He landed so heavily on his *D*s that they completely wiped out his *TH*s, and some of his *R*s must have migrated to Texas where people "warsh" their cars. "This is a very nice place you got here," he said.

"It's not mine." I jerked my thumb at Al, who'd followed me down the hall. "It's his."

"I see," he said, looking Al up and down. Then he gestured to his partner. "This is Special Agent Packard, and I'm Special Agent LeJeune."

At first I thought I'd misheard him, and it wasn't because of the accent. I glanced at Al standing in the hallway, who gave me an almost imperceptible shake of the head. He'd heard the agent's name too. There are coincidences and then there are *coincidences.*

"Mr. Richards, may we come in?" asked the agent.

"Yeah," I said.

Packard followed LeJeune inside, and I shut the door. Packard was young with blond, curly hair and looked a little less savvy than his counterpart. You could always tell a rookie when you saw one. Packard nodded to me but didn't speak.

Second banana, I thought. *What are these guys up to?*

"Mr. Richards?"

"Yeah . . . umm, yes," I corrected myself, not wanting to sound disrespectful. "What can I do for you?"

"Maybe we could sit down?" LeJeune hinted.

"Sure," I said, pointing the way to the formal living room directly off the front entryway.

The two agents walked slowly into the sitting room, scrutinizing the house—just like good cops. They positioned themselves across from each other, the man who called himself LeJeune on the couch facing the hallway toward the kitchen and the other agent, Packard, standing in front of the massive rock fireplace, facing the other way so that they could watch each others' back.

"We'd like to talk about what happened on the slopes today," said LeJeune. "After I heard about it I wanted to meet you," he added, sounding like he was quoting a bad gangster movie.

"I'll bet," I said, nodding.

LeJeune laughed a little and cleared his throat. Packard's face was like a stone.

"I understand you're a police officer in Salt Lake City," LeJeune said.

"Yes, a patrolman," I answered.

"Patrol officer," he corrected. "I'm working on my political correctness. It's only fair." LeJeune chuckled.

The tall agent, Packard, apparently wasn't thrilled with LeJeune's jovial manner and didn't even crack a smile. LeJeune looked at Packard and shook his head. "Anyway, I was just curious about you," LeJeune went on. "We've been working in the Salt Lake area for a couple of months now, you know, with the Olympics around the corner."

"Yeah, I heard about that," I said, and hoped I didn't sound flippant. I didn't mean to.

"Yeah, I guess so. Well, when we heard there might be a killer on the loose, we got real interested, see."

"I can explain," I said. "It was—"

"Raymond Hunt?" he cut in.

"Yeah, how did you know?"

"I'm in investigations." LeJeune laughed again and looked at Packard, who still didn't think anything was funny.

"Right. Anyway, I suppose you know he killed one of our officers, and today I thought I saw him on the ski hill up at Park City. It didn't turn out to be who I thought it was." I thought my candor would hurry these discomforting people out of the house.

"Tell me more about Hunt," LeJeune said, dashing my hopes.

"What don't you know?" I looked in LeJeune's eyes for any clue as to what he was up to.

"You got me there." LeJeune looked at Packard, who didn't even flinch. "I've reviewed his record. You probably know everything I was able to find out. Pretty boy looks, a military background, did some time with a sniper unit."

I nodded as LeJeune described Hunt's background. I'd been over it in my head a hundred times.

"He also did some special training," LeJeune continued, "in demolitions. He got the boot from the military and took up murder instead."

"Wait a minute, did you say demolitions?"

"Yeah, why?"

"Nothing. That's just something new to me." I looked at Al, who shrugged.

"I'll have copies of my information sent to your department if you want."

"That's great, but I don't think anyone is looking into Hunt now."

"Maybe not," said LeJeune. "Anyway, I'd like to hear your version of what happened with Hunt at the refinery. I have the report, but there's no substitute for talking to the source."

I was probably the best source, since I'd been right there. "Hunt escaped from the state pen and ended up hiding in a refinery in Woods Cross, just north of Salt Lake. He took a hostage and shot one of our officers," I provided.

LeJeune nodded his head.

"We never got Hunt," I said flatly.

LeJeune paused for a minute and looked down at the carpet. "Hunt didn't die in the culvert?" he said as if it were a rhetorical question.

I answered anyway. "Not that I know." I looked LeJeune squarely in the eye. He knew as well as I did that Hunt's body was never found.

LeJeune held my stare for a few seconds and then nodded. "Yeah, you got a point, Owen. You really thought it was him? On the ski slope today?"

"Yeah. Well, no," I said after a pause, "I guess not. I did at first, but . . . I made an honest mistake." I didn't feel as sure about my answer as I wanted to. I wasn't all that sure about anything anymore, but it was bad form to equivocate in front of the FBI. Besides, I wanted to know what was up with this LeJeune guy. There must have been hundreds of LeJeunes in the world, but this wasn't the best day for that name to pop up in my life.

LeJeune and his tight-lipped partner seemed satisfied with my story. After being asked a few more cursory questions, I escorted the special agents to the door and we said our good-byes. Actually, Packard just nodded and took one final suspicious glance around the house.

"Mr. Richards," Special Agent LeJeune said, "you let me know if you see this Hunt character around. I mean, it wouldn't do for this bozo to show up on my watch. You get my drift?"

"I'll let you know," I promised. I couldn't tell if LeJeune was patronizing me or being sincere.

They turned to leave, but I couldn't let LeJeune get away without asking something. "Oh, one more thing," I said.

"Yeah." LeJeune turned around in the entryway.

"Uh, your name? You said it was LeJeune?"

"Oh, yeah, sure . . . LeJeune. Why?"

"You don't happen to be French Canadian, by chance, do you?"

"Yeah, you got a good ear for accents," he said in his New York brogue, laughing. Packard still didn't smile, and LeJeune finally threw him a disgusted look.

"No, I mean, I can tell you're from Chicago or somewhere, but I wondered where the name came from."

"Chicago?" he yelled. "You're breaking my heart. Now you better apologize or I'm going to have to break your nose."

"Okay, New York."

"That's better," he said, exaggerating his accent just a bit. "You know, you guys from Utah got no room to talk about accents. I can hear you guys coming from down the block, yes sirree bobcat tail, I can." LeJeune's attempt at a Utah accent was a discordant mixture of Robert DeNiro doing Howdy Doody.

"That's not bad," I said, even though it was terrible, "but your grammar is still too good. Actually, I was just asking because I knew a LeJeune once. He was French Canadian."

"You knew a LeJeune, huh? Maybe we'll have to talk. Familial relations—that's what I want to do while I'm assigned to Salt Lake. I thought I'd look up some of my ancestors. Do a little genealogy."

"Well, this is the place," I said.

"Hey, I get it—Brigham Young. Pretty funny."

"There are probably a lot of LeJeune's where you're from, so . . ." I said, opening Al's massive wooden front door.

LeJeune stopped. "Actually, I never met one outside my immediate family."

"Really?"

"I'm Lem LeJeune, the one and only."

"The one and only?" I asked.

"Yup. Thank you for letting us come. We'll be in touch with you again."

LeJeune's partner nodded, his eyes boring into mine.

I bet they will, I thought. *I just bet they will.*

* * *

Amanda, who'd taken refuge in the kitchen during my little interrogation, quizzed me about my visit with the boys from the bureau, but I didn't say much, just laughed it off and changed the subject. We finished our picnic and dessert, and Amanda left early so Al could nap before his graveyard shift, which began at 11:00 P.M. I decided to drive down the canyon and hit the hay too. I had some things to think about.

LeJeune's very name had nearly stopped my heart. It had felt like a cold wind blowing down my neck, and I hadn't been able to shake the chills ever since.

"I guess I'll be going, Al. I'll see you when I see you," I said as I headed out his back door and into the garage. His phone was ringing, and I didn't want to hold him up.

"Sure, I'll see you Owen," he called after me.

I shut the side door to the garage, locking it, and stared into the cold, dark evening.

The freeway was icy in spots, but I managed to make the thirty-minute drive to my condo safely. I turned into the parking lot and backed into my stall. When I approached my front door, I realized that something wasn't quite right. The door was standing ajar, and the doorjamb was splintered.

An ordinary, thinking person would have dialed 911 on their cell phone or gone to the neighbor's house to call the police. I was too angry. This kind of thing just didn't need to happen to me—not today.

I drew my pistol from my fanny pack and stood to the side of the door. Correct police procedure would have been to call in backup, cover all the exits, and order the bad guy out to avoid having to be in harm's way. I wasn't in the mood.

I gently pushed the door open with my left hand. Looking over the sights of my pistol, which was gripped firmly in my right hand, I moved quickly but quietly through the doorway and hugged the wall where the deepest shadows were cast. I took a moment to listen for movement, not hearing anything. I was able to clear the kitchen area just by looking, but I wanted to check behind the couch before I turned my back on the living room and went down the short hallway to the bathroom and two bedrooms.

Stepping softly, heel to toe, I moved to the couch and looked over my pistol to see behind it. There was no one there, but I could see in the darkness that the room had been turned. Couch cushions were strewn about, and the lamp was tipped over. Whoever burglarized my house had very poor manners.

I turned down the hall and cleared the bedrooms and bathroom in a matter of seconds, flinging open closet doors and ripping a shower curtain down by accident. There was no one. I did a secondary search, looking more closely in places a person could be hiding, like under the sink, beds, and in the linen closet. Again, no one.

I didn't want to contaminate the crime scene any more than I already had, so I left my phone where it was on the floor and dialed the department on my cell phone. A few minutes later, a couple of bored swing-shift officers arrived and gave me very little hope of finding whoever did it. They suggested dusting the place for latent fingerprints, but fingerprint dust left an impossible mess. I asked them to dust the door frame and forget it. I knew how many cold burglaries ever got solved by latent fingerprint evidence.

The last thing in the world I wanted to do was clean up the mess left by the intruder, but I spent a couple of hours putting things back together and doing some much-needed cleaning. Nothing seemed to be missing, not even the typically tempting items like the stereo and computer.

I'd just gotten things back together when there was a knock on the door. I answered it and was surprised to see Al's concerned face.

"Is it that late already?" I asked, looking at my watch.

"It's after midnight," Al said, scanning the room with a practiced eye. "It looks like you've been busy."

"I've been straightening up for nearly two hours," I said without much emotion. I'd had about enough for the day.

"It hasn't been your day, has it?" said Al.

"Nope, that it hasn't." I tossed a wet rag into the sink and sat down, offering Al a seat as well.

Al was running his fingers through his hair, a habit that he usually saved for when he was really stressed.

"Hey, it's not that bad. It happens every day," I said.

"What?"

"Burglaries . . . tons of them . . . every day."

"Yeah, but that's not what I came over for," Al said slowly. "I have some bad news."

"Great, I could use a little bad news about now."

"Well, you're not going to like this. I've had a talk with Lieutenant Michaels. He wants to put a written reprimand in your file for your little Hunt sighting. I fought him all the way, but . . ."

"What?" I nearly shot through the roof and into orbit.

"Owen," Al said, putting his hand on my shoulder, "just listen to me for a minute. The patrol commander is just a little nervous about the Olympics and everything else that has to fall into place before the Games. He readily admits that this may not be in your best interest, but he doesn't feel like he can take a chance on anything right now—not even you."

"What does that mean? I have a perfect record with this department. I deserve some trust!"

"When he found out about the incident on the slopes yesterday, he opened your psychological file."

"Oh, I figured as much when the FBI showed up and threw around the name LeJeune."

"Hey bud, no worries. After what you told me about Missouri and the name LeJeune, I did some checking. That FBI guy has been LeJeune ever since he came here. It looks like that's really his name. As far as I can tell, he's legit."

"Legitimate or not, he's got his grubby little hands on my psych file. How can the department do this?"

Al shrugged. "You know the FBI has a lot of pull, especially now after 9-11 and with the Olympics coming up and everything. It's probably a small thing for them to get their hands on a file like that."

"Yeah, no thanks to the department. Special Agent LeJeune probably has my whole psychological profile memorized," I said sourly. "I am now officially a government-certified wing nut."

* * *

The next day I did a more complete inventory of the condo. I couldn't find anything missing, so I called the investigating officer and told him. We decided to call the whole thing a wash and close the investigation. I had more pressing things to think about.

I decided that instead of getting uptight about having a written reprimand in my file, I'd go with the flow and prove to the department that I was mentally stable. I could argue the letter with an appeal, but I definitely wanted to guard against a fit of temper. It bothered me a little that, because the Olympics were just around the corner, my supervisors would be scrutinizing my every move. Manpower would be in short supply, but I figured that if I played it cool, I'd weather the storm and win in the end. And anyway, I'd never been in trouble at work, so a letter in my file for a year didn't amount to much in the big picture.

I still had another day left of my weekend. Police officers don't keep track of their weekends the way normal people do. A Friday is the last day of an officer's workweek, regardless of what day the calendar reads. Monday is always the beginning day. The days between "Friday" and "Monday" are considered the officer's "weekend." Al had suggested that I spend some time at his place in Park City. His lame excuse was that since he was seeing Amanda on a more regular basis, he needed a chaperone. What an idiot. I didn't want to stay at my place though, so I took him up on it. He made me promise that I'd finally do something to get into shape. I told him I would eat his healthy, icky food, work out with him a few times, and ski.

I called Julianna's place in Kansas City. It was early afternoon there, and I was sure she wouldn't be home—but I liked to call anyway. I left a message telling her my plans and Al's home number, and hung up.

Before I left to go up the canyon to Al's, I packed an overnight bag and locked up the house, checking each window to make sure it was secure. The condo manager had come over early and nailed up a temporary doorjamb. A new frame, I was told, was being ordered and would be installed as soon as possible. I examined the frail piece of furring that had been tacked up to hold the door in place and hoped that a stiff breeze didn't blow the whole thing apart. I had the door open and was looking at the marred deadbolt when two male visitors approached.

They were dressed in dark suits and long coats. They didn't look terribly old, but then, everyone was starting to look young to me. I wasn't surprised that they showed up. In fact, I had been expecting a visit like this.

"Hurry up inside," I said before either of them had a chance to say anything. I practically grabbed them by the lapels and dragged them across the threshold. "It scares me to death when you guys just show up like that. Can't you at least dress like regular people and take those badges off?" I was mildly nervous that someone would get suspicious about these guys showing up all the time.

"We're sorry, Owen. You know we're not allowed to do that," the tallest of the two said.

I moved to the window and narrowed the blinds. "Mrs. Warneke didn't see you, did she?"

"No, I don't think Sister Warneke saw anything," Elder Rose said, shaking his head and laughing.

"Are you sure? She's a very nosy neighbor."

Now they were both laughing—at me.

"Okay, okay," I said. "I'm just a little nervous about people finding out."

"We know," said Elder Rose. "That's one of the things we wanted to talk to you about."

"Okay, but I'm headed up the canyon to stay with a friend. Can we make it quick?"

They looked at each other. "Certainly. In fact, the sooner we get going on this, the better. Then you won't have to sneak around on all your friends."

"You mean? . . ."

"Yes, have you thought any more about a date?"

"Look, you know I want to set a baptism date, but there are just so many things that have to fall into place still."

Both elders were looking at me, not saying anything.

"I know, I know," I said. "I'm lame. I promise I'll try to have a date set by the next time we meet."

"Are you going to meet us at church on Sunday?" Elder Rose took a small notebook calendar from an inside pocket of his coat and checked the date.

"I'll be there."

"Great," he said, slipping the notebook back into his pocket.

Both men said their good-byes, and we shook hands. They walked into the parking lot, but I didn't see them get into a car. With their black trench coats swinging behind them as they walked, they seemed to just fade away, like heaven's servants.

It was hard for me to believe that men so young could hold the keys to so many of life's tough questions. Yet time after time, they answered the deepest theological queries with eloquent simplicity. One of my fears about Mormonism was that, to me, organized religion had always seemed too complicated and political. I learned from Elder Rose and Elder Cannon that I was wrong. They taught me that the truth was always beautiful and exquisitely simple.

* * *

I drove up the mountain and arrived at Al's home in time for lunch. Al, who worked the 11:00 P.M. to 7:00 A.M. shift, wasn't awake yet, so I made myself at home. I honored Al's diet by eating a mound of brown rice and several grilled chicken breasts that were in the fridge, guiltily noting that I was probably only supposed to eat one.

It was a perfect day for skiing. The sun was shining, and it was just below freezing. The powder on top of the mountain would be perfect. I looked out the picture window toward the ski resorts and saw that everyone else seemed to be thinking the same thing, because the hill was covered with people. I decided not to brave the crowds.

I spent the afternoon rattling around in Al's big house while he slept off his graveyard fatigue. I patronized the pool table room and the two-hundred-square-foot weight room complete with sauna. Since I'd learned how to use the remote, I watched his big-screen TV and sampled all of the five hundred channels he received, eventually discovering there was nothing good on. I even took a dip in the covered hot tub in the backyard.

I was soon bored and wandered into Al's comfortable den to find something productive to do. The loveseat was leather, just like the captain's chair behind the wide oak desk, and the artwork featured fly fishermen and kayaking scenes. I had always pictured Al as more of a tennis-racket-and-crossed-oars kind of man.

Seeing Al's computer reminded me to check my e-mail. I rarely received anything of any importance, but occasionally Julianna would pop me a note. Then I would have to call her cell phone and interrupt her at work or class just to hear her melodious voice. I turned the monitor toward me and fingered the keyboard for a few minutes.

I wasn't a complete clod when it came to computers, but I came awfully close. After about three minutes, I'd exhausted my vast computer knowledge just trying to get past Al's screen saver, which taunted me with image after image of scenic photos that I couldn't seem to make go away.

"I knew there was a reason I hated computers," I mumbled as I pounded random keys. Throwing up my hands, I made a mental note to ask Al how his system worked.

The rest of the afternoon passed without me having to help much. I fixed a snack, unable to avoid the really healthy food in Al's fridge, and read a magazine about Park City. Although everyone knew that Park City was an old mining town, I had no idea how extensive the mining had been around the turn of the century.

Al eventually woke up, and I could hear him upstairs in his private suite.

I was relaxing on the sectional when he stumbled into the kitchen, and I looked at him over a log-home magazine. His hair was in a frenzy, and there was white paste around his mouth. He looked like he'd had a rare good day's sleep. "Mornin', handsome," I teased. "I decided to take you up on your offer."

He acknowledged me with a nod and headed for the fridge for a glass of water. I patted my hair to suggest that he needed to flatten a stubborn tuft. He flattened and flattened as I shook my head, and then he gave up with a caustic wave of his hand and a critical stare.

"You look . . . well, you'd have to see it to appreciate it," I remarked.

Al grunted. "You should talk, black-eye boy. You want to do a little workout?" he asked, finishing his water.

"Sure. I tried out the weights a little while ago, but didn't accomplish much. You want to eat something first?"

"Just enough to get the ol' motor some fuel," he said.

"You're a fanatic."

"I've been called worse. Don't worry there, big boy. Right after our workout I'll fix you a good, healthy meal."

"Yum, pine nuts and tofu." I rubbed my stomach.

Al took a few handfuls of peanuts and raisins, and we walked down the stairs to the weight room, where I started my second workout of the day.

I had always teased Al about his fitness fixation, but you can't argue with success. He was doing pretty well considering he wasn't an eighteen-year-old kid anymore.

We made our way to the workout room, where Al set me up for twenty minutes of punishment on the treadmill.

"A couple more hard minutes," Al said after eighteen tough ones.

"Easy for you to say, ape man," I huffed.

"Oh, if you only knew," Al returned.

I pushed myself through the last couple minutes of sprinting before I pulled the emergency cord and let the machine slow to a stop. I threw a towel around my neck and sat down on a bench.

"So, when was the last time you heard from Julianna?" asked Al.

"A week ago, I guess," I said, panting and wiping the perspiration from my face with my towel. "I've been trying to call her. How about messages? Do messages count?"

"No." Al took a gulp of water, spilling on the front of his shirt. "You know it's not easy for someone like her to get attached to someone outside of her religion," he said, leaning against the weight rack.

"Well, that's just what I want to hear." I swiped again at my forehead with my towel and took a long swig of bottled water.

"Just making conversation."

I made one last attempt to dry my face and wrapped the towel around my neck again. "Actually, one of the things I like about Julianna is her . . ." I tried to think of the right words. "Her commitment to principles . . . stuff like that."

"Sounds like you admire more than her striking red hair. Maybe you ought to take a look at what makes her tick."

Al didn't know it, but that's exactly what I had done. My time with Julianna and my strange experience in Missouri had driven me straight to the Mormon missionaries when I got back to Salt Lake. I'd been seeing them for several months and had taken all their discussions. I'd even attended church with them.

Lewis's death and my experience in Missouri had raised a lot of questions. The most significant for me was, why? Why life? What was our ultimate purpose? No fireworks went off when I got the answer from the missionaries, but ideas I'd had for a long time fell into place. Since that time, a lot of things seemed to make more sense. I even felt good about the baptismal challenge the elders had proposed. But I wanted that decision to be mine alone. When the time was right, I'd know. I was sure I would.

"Well, maybe so. That reminds me," I said, trying to change the subject, "are you working tonight?"

"Yup, tonight's my Friday. Amanda's coming over tomorrow," Al said, "and we're going to do some shopping."

"You must have done something very evil to be punished like that on your day off, especially right after working a graveyard shift."

"It must be love. And besides, like you wouldn't trot all the way to Missouri if Julianna wanted you to take her shopping?"

I looked at the treadmill and said, "I *will* be able to trot all the way to Missouri if I keep running on that thing."

The phone rang then and ended our little conversation. Al jogged down the hall and answered it. "Owen," I heard him call.

The only person I knew who'd call me here was Julianna.

I walked to where Al was waiting with the phone in his hand and a puzzled look on his face. He handed me the phone with a shrug.

"Hello?" I said. There was silence for a moment. Al headed up the stairs toward the family room and kitchen.

"Hello?" Still nothing, but something about the sound of the connection told me that the line was open and someone was on the other end.

"Thought you had me, didn't you, pig?" said a rough voice.

"What? Who is this?"

"Maybe you want to try again? Huh, pig?"

"Who is this?"

The line was disconnected with a loud click.

"Al, Al!" I yelled, bounding up the stairs. "Who was that?"

"Don't know," Al said as I rounded the corner into the kitchen. "All it says on the caller I.D. is *Unavailable.*"

Al was filling two glasses with ice water. "Who was it?" he asked, handing me a glass dripping with condensation.

"I don't know. What did he say when you answered?"

"He just asked for you. Nothing special. Why? What's the matter?"

I was a little shaken, and it must have shown in my face.

"I think I just got a call from Raymond Hunt."

* * *

An hour later, Al and I had finished a quick dinner and were sitting in the family room just looking at each other. The weather had changed just as drastically as the mood of the day. A storm front had moved in, and it was starting to snow. Al looked out the window and then at me. He was worried, and I was upset. I tried to blow off the whole thing, but the phone call had really bothered me. I had friends who would move heaven and earth to pull one over on me, but I didn't know anyone who would do something as tasteless as what had just taken place.

"I'm sure it's someone at work," Al offered. "You know how it is. They don't always think about what they're doing. Besides, there are only a handful of people who know about . . ." Al didn't finish.

"About my psychological profile?" I said bitterly.

"I'll ask around. I've got to get to work a little early." Al looked at his watch. "It's after six; I better get going. I've got a sergeant's meeting at seven. I'll be back around eight tomorrow morning. You can help me stay awake until Amanda gets here. Oh, and if it keeps snowing like this, the kid next door will be getting into the garage to get a shovel. He knows the code to the keyless entry. I give him five bucks per blizzard to clear the driveway and the sidewalk."

"I'd do it for half that," I offered.

"Well, you're not a nerdy fifteen-year-old whose mother

wants him to spend a little less time at the computer and a little more time in the harness."

"You need a little brother, don't you?"

"No, you're enough trouble all by yourself," said Al, laughing. "The kid's name is Calvin. He's a good guy. Make him some hot chocolate or something."

"Will do." *I could use some chocolate*, I thought.

Al got up and made for the door. "Take it easy tonight. Make the most of the rest of your weekend. You might not get a lot of time off during the next few weeks."

"You know it."

Al left through the door to the garage, closing it on the way out. I let out a sigh, glad that I wasn't bouncing around my lonely little condo but a little uncomfortable to be taking advantage of Al's hospitality. Al needed a chaperone like I needed another embarrassing incident in my life, but I appreciated his kindness.

The back door opened up again and Al poked his head in the doorway. I could hear his Subaru idling in the driveway.

"Hey, check your e-mail," he said. "I forwarded you a good picture of Edgar."

The door shut before I could tell Al that I couldn't get past his screen saver. I decided not to bother him with it tonight. Photos of Edgar Martinez, the famed Seattle Mariner designated hitter, could wait.

Calvin showed up just after Al left. I opened the front door in time to see him dragging a shovel out of the garage. I waved, and he gave me what could have been called a nod if you counted the almost imperceptible swaying of the bangs that hung over his eyes. He managed to put the working end of the shovel on the driveway and began the painstakingly slow drudgery of scraping a light dusting of snow off the concrete.

"Hey, Cal," I said, hoping that I'd sound hip, or rad, or whatever the kids said these days.

Calvin gave me another one of his patented micronods and continued to push his shovel. I shook my head and went back inside the warm house, knowing that Calvin would never see me through the jungle of hair that swung in front of his face anyway. From inside of the house, I could hear his shovel making pass after slow pass across the driveway.

"A picture of Edgar, huh?" I said. Al, one of those weird Oakland A's fans, knew my weakness for Seattle Mariner baseball. I decided I wanted to see what kind of picture moved him to think of me. Besides, there might be something in my box from a certain redheaded siren.

I sat in Al's leather swivel chair and faced the computer, clicking on the keys and once again trying to figure out what kind of magical touch would disable the screen saver. I spun in the chair. "Nothing," I said, frustrated beyond belief.

The relentless scraping sound of Calvin's shovel had moved out to the sidewalk, but it gave me an idea.

I opened the front door and yelled for him. His head came up (a good sign), and he brushed the hair from his face, revealing a set of eyes complete with eyebrows.

"Yeah?" he said.

"Come here for a minute."

He looked at the half-finished sidewalk and reluctantly dropped his shovel, making his way to the front door.

"Yeah?" he said as he neared.

Calvin, under the mop of hair, was a good-looking boy with surprisingly intelligent eyes. His facial features were sharp and promised to mature into a handsome mug. Someday he'd get a haircut, move out of his T-shirt, and impress somebody.

"Calvin, I'm Owen Richards. I'm staying here for a few days. What does Al pay you for shoveling the walks?" I asked him.

"Five bucks," he said glumly.

"How about if I double that if you help me with his computer?"

I couldn't have gotten a better reaction if I'd inserted a boot disk up his nose and typed the command "Show glee." He glanced furtively towards his house, no doubt suppressing a small amount of guilt for violating his computer downtime, and jumped into the entryway. I pointed in the general direction of the den, and Calvin went for the computer like a hound on a scent.

He found his way to the chair and rolled it squarely in front of the keyboard.

"What can I do for you?" he asked, using a complete sentence for perhaps the first time that month.

"Uh, I can't make it work. I mean, I can't get on-line."

"Child's play," he said, striking the space bar. A dialogue box came up asking for a password. "What's the password?"

"I don't know. I couldn't even get in that far," I said.

Calvin had flipped his long bangs over the top of his head, so I could see when his eyebrows went up in anticipation. "You want me to break in?" he asked hopefully.

"Okay."

"Okay, you want me to break into it?" he asked. "Or, that's okay, you don't want me to?"

"Okay, I want you to fudge past that password and help me get on-line so I can check my e-mail."

"You are being intentionally vague," he said, surprising me with a five-syllable word and impeccable pronunciation. "Breaking in is breaking in, in any language, and euphemistic talk won't get you into this computer."

I just stared at Calvin, working hard to keep my jaw from dropping. The kid had a real live vocabulary and hadn't called me "dude" once.

"Break in," I finally said.

"Break in?"

"Break in."

"Cool," he said, attacking the keys at the speed of light.

Several minutes later, Calvin relinquished his seat in front of the computer, and I scrolled through the e-mails looking for the one from Al. When I found it, Calvin was looking over my shoulder, waiting to see what had been so important.

Al's message was called, appropriately, *Enfuego*. The picture was of Edgar Martinez midswing, completely engulfed in fire. Super cool.

Another e-mail, addressed to me without a subject line, caught my attention, and I clicked it. The file opened, and I read the very short message. My first reaction was disbelief followed by gut-wrenching anger. My eyes, wide open like my mouth, locked on the message long enough to get a reaction from Calvin. I soon convinced him that the message was merely an inside joke, and then tried to convince myself.

The e-mail made its point in just one succinct sentence.

A man can only die once.
Raymond Hunt

CHAPTER 4

I didn't touch the computer except to print the message and disconnect with Al's Internet service. I ushered Calvin out with a ten-dollar bill and then sat up for a while wondering what to do. I tried without success to fall asleep in the guest room in Al's basement.

I must have slept a little because I was startled awake by a noise. It didn't seem like the right time for Al to be home, but I could hear his footsteps in the hallway upstairs near the kitchen. He usually took his shoes off, but I figured he was probably tired. I scavenged on the floor for my watch and pushed the button to illuminate the face. It was 4:00 A.M. He'd gone in early, so I assumed he'd left work at three to minimize overtime accrual.

I threw the covers off and stepped unsteadily out of bed and into the hall.

"Al?" I called out softly, unsure of why I was whispering. It wasn't like I was going to wake anyone.

There was no answer. I heard some more soft noises, and then everything was quiet.

"Al?" I asked again into the dark. I'd probably missed him. If he felt like I did after a night shift, he was too tired to bother with anything but finding his pillow.

I went back into my room, closing the door behind me. I hit the pillow and thought I would fall straight to sleep, but it didn't happen. There was too much going on in my head.

I heard a few more soft noises, and then the house quieted down again. Sometime in the next hour I fell into a fitful sleep.

I was awakened later by more noise. I reluctantly rolled over and looked at the clock. Eight in the morning. I hauled my sleepy carcass out of bed and made my way up the stairs to the kitchen.

"Hey, man, what are you doing up?" I asked when I saw Al standing at the counter.

"Long night," Al said, rubbing his temples.

"So, what are you doing up?"

"I'm getting ready to pound down some serious breakfast," Al said. He was wearing a sweat-stained T-shirt that was wrinkled where his ballistic vest went over it.

"How long have you been home?"

"I just got in."

"You mean you came home at four and left again?"

"No, I mean I came home and now I'm going to eat," he said, and I could tell he was a little irritated with my interrogation.

"You didn't come home at four?" I asked, slightly panicked.

"No, I just got here. At four I was in a Denny's restroom with a handful of green hair from some punk who got off the fashion train a decade ago and never made it back on."

"No, really. I heard someone in the house at about four this morning."

"You must have been dreaming," said Al.

"Well, I wasn't dreaming, and I certainly didn't dream this." I picked up a paper off the counter and handed him the e-mail message I'd printed the night before.

"So, what do you think?" I asked after he'd read it.

"Let's get that FBI guy in on this right away."

"Great—one more nail in my coffin."

Al ignored me and moved toward the phone. "I'll get dispatch to call—"

"It's kind of early," I interrupted him.

"It's after eight. What's the matter, Owen?"

"Nothing. Go ahead," I acquiesced.

Al dialed the phone and spoke with one of the dispatcher. He waited on the phone for quite a while before he spoke again. Apparently he'd been forwarded to LeJeune himself, and after a brief explanation, he said a couple of uh-huhs and hung up.

"Look at it this way," Al said. "Now you've got proof that you're not cracking up."

"Hey, goody for me," I said. "So, what did LeJeune say?"

"He's on his way up with a technician to check out the computer. He said not to change anything. Let's eat."

Al went to the kitchen and broke out two pounds of bacon, a dozen eggs, and a bag of potatoes. I thought I was seeing things.

"What's all this?" I asked, wide-eyed.

"What does it look like? It's breakfast." He tossed me a grater and told me to make myself useful with the spuds.

"What happened to the power oatmeal and cottage cheese? Where's the ground wheat mush and egg whites?"

"It's my Saturday. When are you going to learn to eat like a man?"

Al ate like there were no more eggs in the world. I ate as if I wouldn't see that kind of food ever again, which was a distinct possibility living with Al, the good-for-you-food king.

It didn't take long for LeJeune to arrive. He brought with him a thin, humorless man wearing wire-framed glasses and sporting a funny little mustache that just tickled his top lip.

"This is Special Agent Papadakos," LeJeune said by way of introduction. "He's a technology specialist."

"Nice to meet you," I said, holding out my hand.

LeJeune let out smug laugh. "It's like having my own private computer Greek."

I looked at Papadakos to see if he was going to punch LeJeune in the mug, but he was laughing.

"It's okay," LeJeune said. "He's immune to my humor. So, tell me what you've got here."

I handed over the printed copy of the e-mail. LeJeune studied it and then handed it to Papadakos, who took the paper and turned away from us as if to get a little privacy.

"You've had a rough week, Mr. Richards." LeJeune got right to the point. "What can you tell me?"

Al interrupted. "I'll show Special Agent Papadakos to the computer."

"This kind of job is what he dreams of," LeJeune said of Papadakos as they walked toward the den. He took off his coat and looked at me, waiting for me to say something.

"At first I thought the ski hill and the burglary were just ugly coincidences," I said. "Now I'm not so sure." I thought about the noises I'd heard during the night, but decided not to say anything about it, figuring I was getting a little too paranoid. We walked into the living room and sat down. I had the manners of a goat, so LeJeune just draped his coat over the arm of a chair.

"Do you get along with everyone at work?" he asked, taking out a small spiral notebook and pen.

"I always have."

LeJeune took a few notes. I'd done the same thing a thousand times and never thought about how it made a person feel. Suddenly I realized how disconcerting it was. I watched

LeJeune scribble for a few moments, wondering how he was going to characterize this visit.

"It may be your friends," he said, looking up from his notebook. "They get a little . . . funny sometimes?"

"I thought maybe the phone call last night was a joke."

"What phone call?" LeJeune set the notebook in his knee.

"Last night at about five-thirty or six, I guess. I got a call from some guy."

LeJeune went back to his pen and pad. I told him about the call while he wrote. He asked all the standard questions about speech characteristics of the caller, background noise, and specific words used—everything I would have asked.

"Any bad guys released from jail or prison lately who might have it out for you?" he asked.

"I have no idea," I said. "I don't keep track of stuff like that."

He scribbled some more, obviously deep in thought. When he finished, he lowered the notebook and looked up. His eyes drilled straight into mine.

"Who's doing this?" he asked.

I started to tell him that I didn't know, but his eyes were still locked on mine, and that answer didn't seem like enough.

"I mean," said LeJeune, dropping his gaze, "if you were to guess, who do you think is likely to do this?"

"You mean besides Raymond Hunt?"

"I haven't ruled him out yet," LeJeune pointed a finger at me, "but yeah, besides Hunt. Who would do this to you?"

"Nobody."

"Okay," said LeJeune, "then let's say this is about Hunt. Why would he be doing this to you?"

"Well," I said slowly, "I was the team leader of the unit that drove him out of the refinery. I saw him with the hostage, and I saw him shoot Lewis." I looked around the room, trying to think about what might have triggered Hunt and made him fixate on me. "I was also a witness at the coroner's inquest after they said he'd died," I finished.

Al came back into the room just then, leaving the computer in Papadakos's capable hands. "I can tell you why he would do this," he said, turning to look at LeJeune. "Owen was the primary witness at the inquest—the only one to bring up any doubt about Hunt's death. A lot of experts testified about how unlikely it was for a person to survive in that culvert. The Hunt family had a lot riding on the outcome of that trial. Hunt's mother stood to receive a fortune in life insurance benefits, and they were gearing up to sue the city and the department for wrongful death. If the judge had come back with a finding that Hunt had actually died, the Hunt family would have had stronger grounds for a suit."

I nodded. "I wasn't very popular with the family in the courtroom."

"That's an understatement." Al moved to a chair and sat. "The inquest should have lasted a couple of hours, but it went on for nearly two full days. Hunt's mother practically assaulted Owen in the hallway outside the courtroom. The bailiff almost arrested her."

"There were some hard feelings," I said.

"Hard feelings?" Al went on. "What was it you called Mrs. Hunt—"

"Okay, more than hard feelings," I interrupted. Turning to LeJeune, I said, "The judge at the inquest was just about to rule in favor of an accidental death finding. The Hunt family attorney was arguing for a finding of justifiable homicide, which might have been fine if they'd had a body, but Hunt's body was never found. I simply kept reminding people of that, and . . ."

"Reminding?" Al said. "You nearly got yourself thrown out of the courtroom for contempt of court. You can't call a judge a—"

"Never mind," I said. I wasn't thrilled with the way Al's version of the truth was coming out. If LeJeune was working on the theory that Lewis's death had thrown me into a psychotic tailspin, Al's interpretation of the events at the inquest was not going to help my case.

"Look," I said to Al, "I know that it seemed like I took Lewis's death pretty hard, but give me a break. He was a close friend—almost like a brother. Besides, the judge did come around in the end, and the cause of Hunt's death was never officially verified. Hunt is still officially only *presumed* dead."

I looked at LeJeune to see if I could read a reaction on his face. He was looking at us with interest, but his thoughts were hidden behind a mask of amusement.

"So, the Hunt family never got their big payoff," said LeJeune.

"Kind of a weak motive," I offered.

"Well, it may be," LeJeune said, "but in the end, it always has to do with money." He made a few more notes in his little book and looked up. "Or maybe Hunt is just a psychopath."

There was no doubt in my mind that Hunt was a dyed-in-the-wool psychotic, but I also knew that I'd offended Hunt's family at the inquest, and I'd been a real pain in the process. It wouldn't have surprised me if Hunt was doing this to me for that very reason. What concerned me even more was that I didn't know if LeJeune could be convinced of the same thing. I doubted it. The FBI would never concern itself with something like this if it weren't for the Olympics.

"At this point," said LeJeune, "the press covering the Olympics hasn't picked this up, and I doubt anyone is taking much notice of it. It's a small thing, relatively speaking." I appreciated LeJeune's candor, but it sounded like I was more interested in solving the mystery than he was. "My job," LeJeune continued, "is to make sure this doesn't turn into a big thing."

LeJeune fixed me with a reassuring look. Maybe he did care. Papadakos made his way quietly from the den and cleared his throat, breaking LeJeune's stare.

"Do you fellas mind?" asked LeJeune, gesturing toward Papadakos and the den. They retreated into the den for some privacy.

Neither Al nor I said anything. We both just sat there, letting our private theories run in our heads.

LeJeune came back to the living room shaking his head. "Computer guys." He sat down again as if we were in for a long wait, then looked back and forth between Al and me. "Let's see if we can make sure the Olympics aren't interrupted by a special national news broadcast. If there's a wacko running loose around Park City, my job is to figure out if it's the cop-killing psychopath," he gestured to his notebook, where he'd written all the facts about Hunt, "or just a nut-case cop." He looked straight at me.

LeJeune had an extraordinary way with words, but at least I didn't have to wonder what he was thinking. I wasn't delighted that the Feds thought of me as a nut-case cop, but in a begrudging way, I appreciated LeJeune's honesty. I folded my arms and sat quietly.

"You don't have to be helpful, but it wouldn't hurt. I have to ask you some questions you won't like. Do you want to get it over with?"

"Why not?" I asked.

"I have to wonder," said LeJeune. "Sometimes these things just have a sense of timing that is purely their own, yet sometimes that timing is everything."

Al and I looked at each other, not sure what he was getting at.

"Let me put it a better way." He sat up in his chair. "If this is the work of some freak of nature, then the timing might not mean anything—it might not matter that the Olympics are coming up. But from what I know about Hunt, he's sophisticated enough to plan something like this around events in *your* life. Understand?"

"Sure," I said, "but I can't think of anything special going on in my life right now."

"No big event or change? No major problem you're dealing with right now?"

I thought for a moment. "No, nothing."

"What about Julianna?" asked Al.

"She couldn't possibly have anything to do with this. She's more than a thousand miles away." I shook my head, and Al shrugged. I kept thinking.

LeJeune was patient for a few minutes, then asked, "So, who is Julianna? Girlfriend?"

"Uh," I thought about it for a second, "just a girl . . . I mean, she's a friend. Kind of a girl, a friend, sort of."

LeJeune smiled and looked at Al. "I see," he said. "What's the matter? Love life not going so good, eh?"

"It's hard to understand if you don't understand the . . ." I thought quickly how to phrase it, "the unique culture of Utah," I finished, now totally embarrassed.

"What can't I understand?" he asked.

"It's nothing. Never mind." The last thing in the world I needed was advice for the lovelorn from this Big Apple Cupid.

"What? Because I talk like your Uncle Vito and I didn't grow up on a one-acre plot in the land of milk and honey, you assume I don't know anything about The Church of Jesus

Christ of Latter-day Saints?" LeJeune gave us a smug look.

"No way." I was shocked.

"Way. And before you make another assumption, I'm not a convert either."

"That's not so unusual," I said, even though it did seem a little odd to me. But then, what did I know about things?

"In fact," said LeJeune, settling in for what promised to be a fascinating story, "I'm at least a fifth generation member of the Church *and* a fifth generation New Yorker. Now that *is* unusual."

I nodded.

"What do you mean, *at least* fifth generation?" asked Al.

"I'll tell you, Al," said LeJeune, gesturing into the air. LeJeune's New York accent thickened. "My genealogy goes back to these mountains and this valley," he said, looking out over Park City through Al's big windows. "My great-great-grandfather was orphaned in this valley in '49—that's 1849. He was a toddler. No one knows his birth date because his parents both died on the trip west. All the LeJeune journal says is that this little kid was left alone on the trail after an accident with the wagons. A man named LeJeune and his wife took him in as part of their family. That's where the LeJeune name comes from."

Al nodded, obviously intrigued by this story of the hardships and sacrifices of the first Mormons. He was also interested, as I was, with this pioneer named LeJeune.

"It wasn't such a big deal. Great-great-grandfather LeJeune married a widow with a son. I guess he figured, 'What's one more mouth to feed?'"

As LeJeune went on, a tingle crept up my spine. Until talking to Al, I'd never told anyone about Bart LeJeune.

LeJeune continued. "The baby took his new father's name, LeJeune. So, this little kid grows up and wonders who his real family is. Naturally, as soon as he's of age, he heads his horse's snout east and rides off to the Big Apple to find his roots."

"I think pigs have snouts. I don't know what a horse has," I said.

"Nostrils?" said Al.

"Whatever, anyway," LeJeune said, "it's all recorded in the LeJeune journals. The little orphan never lost his faith, but he never returned to the West either. Until yours truly, that is."

"Did he ever hook up with members of his biological family?" Al asked.

"Not a one. He kept great records of his own adopted family after that. But he never really found any of his family back east."

"So, you're going to solve the mystery?" said Al.

"I'm just a bum from Queens, but I'm working on it," LeJeune said. "The leads, they get pretty cold after a hundred years." He chuckled at himself.

"What kind of leads do you have?" I said.

"My adoptive great-grandmother was a close friend of my real great-grandmother. From the records she kept, we—my wife and I—were able to identify the family of the adopted boy."

"That's something," said Al. "You're in the right place to pick at that thread. There's no bigger repository of genealogy than right here in Salt Lake."

"But the irony is that in her journal, Great-grandmother LeJeune goes on and on about my biological great-grandmother's extensive genealogical records, journals, and pictures."

"Pictures?" said Al. "Isn't all this a little too far back in history to be talking about photographs?"

"Drawings, sketches. Go figure—she was big into art. Great-grandmother LeJeune said Rebecca—that's my real great-grandmother's name—sketched everything that moved, and half the things in the world that didn't. She'd drawn everything ever since she was a little girl in Far West. Can you imagine who might be in those drawings?"

When LeJeune mentioned the little girl in Far West who drew pictures, my blood turned to ice. What was until a few minutes ago the world's biggest coincidence was now downright spooky. No one on this earth could have known about the little girl in Far West who asked to draw my picture when I was there. There was no way LeJeune could have known about her.

"So, you have a Rebecca who likes to draw," said Al. "But you don't have the family records?"

"Not nearly enough of them," said LeJeune. "It would have been something to see a drawing of good ol' Bartoleme LeJeune, and his wife, Anna, too."

"Bartoleme?" I said. *Bartolome?*

"Yeah, Bartoleme as in Bart. That's my name, too. I go by Lem. You think I want to go around with a name like Bart all my life? Now, Lem—there's a name with some class." LeJeune adjusted his tie and put his nose in the air. "They're up here, you know," he continued.

"Who's up here?" I asked.

"The journals and the pictures. They were left in the wreckage of the wagon accident. Leaving the records up here in the mountains didn't sit too well with Anna."

"Why didn't somebody pick them up? That seems like a pretty valuable item to leave behind."

"Old Bart was used to being in charge, and I guess he just didn't want to hold up the wagon train while he roped down to the wreckage to pick through the wagon. It had been hard enough bringing the bodies up out of the canyon—he was just plain stubborn, if you ask me."

"I'll say," I spoke up. "I remember once that ornery old cuss told me to—"

"What was that, Owen?" asked Al, loud enough to shut me up. He stared at me with a disturbed look on his face.

"Huh? Oh, nothing. I meant, yeah, he sounds stubborn. I mean, from what you said . . . and everything." I had just about put my foot in my mouth all the way to my hip flexors.

"Uh, yeah, whatever," said LeJeune. "Anyway, Anna wrote quite a scathing description of her feelings on the matter in her journal. Bart never went back for the stuff. It's a shame—those people are completely helpless unless we find their records someday."

The rest of what LeJeune said went right past me. My experiences in mid-nineteenth century Missouri were intensely personal, so much so that I'd felt some regret telling Al about them, even though I trusted him. But Lem LeJeune's description of his adoptive grandparent was beyond mere coincidence.

"You're kidding," LeJeune said to Al about something I hadn't heard. "Well, enough about me. I have to get back to work." He stood and turned to address me. "Thank you for your time, Owen." He clicked his pen and closed his notebook. "If it means anything to you, my money is on the cop-killing psychopath theory."

"What? Oh yeah, thanks," I said. "What about the e-mail?"

Papadakos, who was just coming out of the den, looked pensively back and forth at Al and me and answered for LeJeune.

"It seems we know where the e-mail came from," he said.

Al and I both sat up in our seats, anxious to hear.

"It seems to have come from a computer in Salt Lake."

"Salt Lake." I nodded, not overly surprised.

"Yeah, Salt Lake. It's your address, Mr. Richards. The e-mail was sent from your very own computer."

"My place?" I gasped. "During the burglary?"

"That's what I was thinking. What were you doing at about 0230 hours on the morning just after the burglary?"

"Two-thirty," I said, looking at Al. "At two-thirty I was there, asleep, or trying anyway. That was well after the burglary."

Al nodded. "I was there about midnight to check on Owen. I left well before two-thirty."

"So you were alone, Mr. Richards?" asked LeJeune. "At two-thirty, you were alone?"

"Yes," I said softly. "Yes, I was."

* * *

I hadn't been taken to jail or hauled off to the loony bin, but I felt like the world's most notorious imbecile. LeJeune had a few more questions for me, and he tried not to make them sound accusatory, but he had a job to do. I'd given Papadakos and him consent to search my condo, specifically my computer, and we agreed to follow them straight to my place.

Al and I went in my truck and met LeJeune and his partner there. After we arrived, LeJeune took a series of digital photos and then threatened to dust the place for prints. I cringed but allowed him to dust anyway. Papadakos didn't waste any time getting to my computer, but rather than looking at it there, he packaged each component as evidence and hauled it off to the trunk of his car.

LeJeune was friendly to the end. He gave me his cell number and told me to call him directly if anything else came up. I think he was hoping I wasn't a tinfoil-hat-wearing nutcase, but the way I felt, a tinfoil hat to protect me from the invisible rays of the martian mother ship didn't sound like a bad idea.

Al stayed close by me at my condo to lend moral support and even offered to make the ultimate "sacrifice" and cancel his shopping date with Amanda. He didn't end up being that lucky because we finished up at the condo in plenty of time to make it back up the canyon. I wasn't anxious to barge in on Al's time with Amanda, but he wouldn't have it any other way. I was officially going on a date with Amanda and Al. What a joy.

When we got back to Al's, Amanda had let herself in and was waiting in the family room reading one of Al's log-home magazines.

Al explained what had happened, and Amanda was more than gracious about letting me tag along. Before the three of us took off on our little shopping date, Al and I went back to his den to check our e-mail accounts, which we were instructed to do as often as possible. Al was hovering over his Hotmail account and asked me for my password.

"It's A-C-H-J-A," I told him.

"What?"

"Ach Ja, you know . . . it's German. It means *oh yeah.* Like, what was that silly password of mine? Oh yeah."

Al shook his head and typed it in.

"Hey, you got a new one."

My neck went rigid.

"Loosen up," said Al. "It's from Julianna. That should brighten up your day a little."

And did it ever. My heart rate doubled, and I had to concentrate on not letting Al see my fervor. "I'll read it later," I said, barely able to contain my breathing. "I don't want to hold everybody up."

Al gave me a disgusted grimace and got up from the seat in front of the desk, directing me to sit down. I gracefully accepted his invitation and walked calmly to the computer, making sure that I didn't seem too anxious. Al just shook his head. Amanda, who was watching quietly from the doorway, wasn't as demure and laughed out loud.

Julianna's e-mail was short but sweet.

> *I tried calling you at Al's but no one was there. I left a bazillion messages on your cell. You know, if you learned how to use your cell phone you could listen to them. I'm coming to Utah for a job interview and maybe to take in a winter game or two. I might need a ride from the airport if you can swing it. I haven't set my travel dates yet. Talk to you soon.*
>
> *Love, Ju*

"Yes!" I shouted. "I mean, uh, okay, you guys ready to go?"

Now they were both laughing at me.

"Well," I said, "I'm not going to let one more minute of prime shopping time go to waste." I trotted out of the den, desperately punching buttons on my cell, trying to access the message log. Technology just hated me.

We shopped for several hours. I don't know how Al put up with it. I, on the other hand, handled it quite well. I was so absorbed in thinking about Julianna that the shopping didn't even bother me. One time Amanda asked me to try something on and learned firsthand my policy on doing it—I simply didn't. She didn't ask again. Al tried things on at every store. Poor Al.

After lunch, I threw cold water on the whole affair by reminding them I had to run down the mountain to work. Al was barely awake from having missed a night's sleep, so

Amanda took pity on him and we all went back to his place. We pulled into Al's driveway, clear of snow from Calvin's good work, and dragged Al into the family room. He was dead on his feet.

I went downstairs to the guest room and pawed through my clean clothes for a T-shirt. I found one and bounded up the stairs into the family room. Amanda was fussing over Al, who was sitting on the couch with his eyes half open.

"Have you seen my hat?" I asked.

"What hat?" Al mumbled.

"My Mariners hat. I wore it yesterday. I know it was here somewhere." I scanned the room and lifted a blanket on the couch.

"If you're going to have an unhealthy fixation on a baseball team, why not choose a real team?"

"One hundred and sixteen games in 2001?" I said, bragging about one of the Mariners' few really outstanding seasons.

Al wasn't paying attention. He was still lounging on the sectional with his eyes closed. "I don't know where it is. It was in the laundry room the last time I saw it, on top of a pile of your ski stuff. Oh, and you can brag when the M's make the big game in October."

I grunted and went into the laundry room to look around. When I came back out, I said, "I can't find it."

"You and your Mariners," Al mumbled.

I looked a few more places around the house and then gave up. I had about forty-five minutes to make it to work.

* * *

After my shift, I was back to Al's place before midnight and crept into the house. Al was already asleep, trying to make the adjustment back to normal daytime hours for the balance of his weekend. I knew how difficult that transition was, so I tiptoed down to the guest room and went to bed. I slept pretty well, despite my woes over not finding my hat. I'd even done a quick check at my place in Salt Lake. It was an original Mariners team hat with the upside down, yellow trident on the front. It may not have been in collector's condition, but it fit my head nicely, and there weren't too many of those caps around.

Al was up before me, and when I awoke, I was looking forward to another big, country-style breakfast.

"What's on the griddle this morning?" I asked, sauntering into the kitchen with my hands on my belly.

Al turned around and slid a bowl of something mushy towards me. It looked nothing like eggs or bacon or even hash browns.

"This looks like . . . wheat crumbs," I said with a frown.

"Good. It's supposed to," said Al.

"But what about yesterday? The eggs? The meat? The grease?"

"That was yesterday," he said. "Today is a new day. No more junk food until my next Saturday."

"But, Al, today *is* Saturday."

"I realize that for other people it's Saturday, but it's my Sunday. And," Al said, "speaking of Sundays, why don't you go to church with me tomorrow morning, on the real Sunday?"

"Does Amanda know about this?" I asked.

"About what?"

"About this bait and switch diet? Are you holding back on her? That's not good in a marriage." I shook my finger at Al.

"Quit trying to change the subject. Are you coming to church with me or not?"

"I . . ." I remembered that I was supposed to meet the missionaries for church in Salt Lake. "I have something I have to take care of in Salt Lake tomorrow."

"Really? What?"

"It's something . . . I set up a long time ago. I can't really back out now. So, what's that wonderful smell?"

"Cottage cheese. You're going to shed a few pounds of fat."

"I'm telling Amanda."

* * *

The weekend passed, and I finished out my workweek still mooching off Al. I might have been *persona non grata* at Park City Mountain Resort, but the wonderful thing about Parley's Canyon was that there was always another resort within a stone's throw. On both my days off I skied without incident and slept in Al's guest room. Working swing shift made it hard to find time to hook up with Julianna by phone, but I was able to sneak in a few calls.

With Al working nights and sleeping days, we only saw each other in the evenings, but I found Al to be a gracious host and easy to get along with. Amanda came for dinner Sunday night, and I saw firsthand that things between them were becoming more serious. Al's days were numbered.

"Have you been checking your e-mails like the federal government directed?" Al asked me one night. He was resting on his couch watching a Jazz game. The house was warm despite the subfreezing temperatures outside. It was dipping below zero most nights, but Al's sturdy, lodge-style home was keeping out the chill.

"I guess I'd better . . . Can you go to a federal pen for failing to obey an agent?" I sauntered into the den and navigated the Internet until my e-mail account came up.

There were four e-mails in the queue; two told me that I'd won a grand prize, and another promised me low interest rates on a second mortgage. I deleted those without opening them. The last one was from Julianna. I clicked it and waited for the computer to think. When the message appeared, I read it with great anticipation. It was good news.

"Julianna arrives in Salt Lake tomorrow morning!" I shouted.

"Great. Bring her up. Maybe she'll bring you a Royal's hat from Kansas City."

"You disgust me," I said, walking back into the family room.

Al stood up and tried to swat me with a pillow, and I made the mistake of grabbing his wrist to prevent getting hit. His reaction was immediate and effective. He stepped back, letting my momentum carry me forward, and at the same time rolled my fist off his arm with his hand. I felt my elbow turn over, and before I could catch myself I was headed for the floor. It all ended with me kissing the carpet and Al kneeling behind my outstretched arm. He gave my wrist one slight twist and I gasped. Then he gently released my arm.

"What in the wide world of sports was that?" I asked, rolling onto my back and shaking the cramp out of my shoulder.

"Ikkyo."

"Gesundheit," I said.

"No, katate dori ikkyo. Like this: ka-tah-tay door-ee ee-key-oh."

"Whatever—it's more of that martial arts stuff you're into. Well, don't even think of trying any more of that Karate Kid stuff on me."

"It's not karate. It's aikido. Nice, huh?"

"That depends on which side of it you happen to be on." I rubbed my shoulder and grimaced.

"It's not hard. Do you want to try it?"

"That stuff is beyond me." I pushed myself up and sat on the couch. "Remember when you threw that one guy at Pioneer Park? That was the most spectacular thing I've ever seen."

"He didn't give me much of a chance. He was coming at me full speed with a rake handle. Besides, I didn't do anything but get out of the way. He provided all the momentum."

Al was a talented martial artist, but we rarely saw him use his stuff on the street. For one thing, he was a good cop and rarely got into brawls. For another, when he did use his martial arts training, the fight always looked so benign that none of us ever even noticed it. All we ever saw was a short scramble followed by a suspect wincing on the wrong end of one of Al's famous wristlocks.

"Well, whatever you did definitely cured him of charging at cops with rake handles."

"I don't think he really wanted to hit me. I just helped him to realize that," said Al. "You know what they say—'The earth is slow, but the oxen are patient.'"

"I'm not even going to ask," I said. "So, show me that sticky-oh thing."

"It's called Ikkyo. Ee-key-oh," Al said, getting up and moving to the center of the family room.

I got off the couch and stood in front of Al. "I'm ready, Sensei."

"Okay, throw a punch. Right here." Al patted his midsection.

I thrust my fist halfheartedly towards his belly, waiting to see what kind of pretzel I was going to end up looking like. Al didn't do anything, and my punch bounced off his stomach.

"You're right," I said, shrugging my shoulders. "I could probably learn that move."

"If that's the hardest you can hit me, then I don't need a martial art to defend myself. Do it again, but this time throw some weight behind it."

I didn't want to hurt Al. "Well, how hard do you want me to hit you?"

"How far do you want to fly?" he said, grinning.

* * *

Al rearranged my shoulders showing me how to do sticky-oh, which I called it over and over until he pinned me to the carpet and made me promise to stop. He was very good. My first lesson taught me a deeper respect for the art. "Simple physics," he'd called it.

I limped to bed early so I could get up and be at the airport before Julianna's flight landed, but I was kidding myself if I thought I was going to fall asleep. I spent most of the night thinking about Julianna and telling myself that I was going to have to be well rested and at my best by morning. When morning did come, I felt a mixture of exhaustion and exhilaration.

I was waiting at the security gate long before her arrival and spent almost an hour fidgeting in an uncomfortable chair. I hadn't seen Julianna since just after Lewis's funeral. We communicated by e-mail and phone and had become good friends, but our relationship wasn't very well defined. I'd never even asked her if she was dating anyone. I knew that most of the people she was apt to meet in Salt Lake with me were going to assume that she and I were an item, and I suppose I hadn't ever really tried to dissuade people of that assumption.

I wriggled in my chair a little. The truth was that Julianna probably just regarded me as the dopey friend of her cousin, which caused me to squirm even more in my chair.

I caught a glimpse of her long, wavy, burnished-amber hair as she passed behind a very large gentleman carrying a briefcase and wearing a business suit that was about three sizes too small for his mammoth girth. The buttons on his jacket had probably never been introduced to the buttonholes on the other side. He walked in front of Julianna, blocking my view until he struggled through a turnstile and headed for another gate. When the eclipse was over, I watched Julianna walk through the turnstile and hoist the strap of a small travel bag over her shoulder. When she saw me in the crowd, her sea-foam green eyes brightened and her smile broadened. Her mere presence made my chest constrict. I couldn't inhale.

"Owen, hello!" she said. She was even more gorgeous close-up, with her flawless porcelain complexion and straight white teeth—almost like an airbrushed picture in a magazine. She wore a brown and tan cable-knit sweater and tan denim pants with leather boots. It wasn't an expensive look, but it was perfect to me.

I just stood there, trying to breathe.

"Owen?" she said.

I opened my mouth, but still, nothing came out.

Julianna leaned toward me and gave me a polite hug. Luckily, it was just enough to squeeze some air out of me and restart my breathing.

I squeaked out a faint hello.

"It's great to see you, Owen. It's been forever."

I took a deep breath that allowed a sufficient amount of oxygen to reach my brain as I thought of a million clever things to say.

"Yeah."

"Oh, what happened to your eye?" she asked, gently prodding my cheek with her finger.

"A little ski accident." I didn't want Julianna to learn the whole ridiculous story. "Let me help you with that," I said, taking her carry-on bag and slinging it over my shoulder.

Whatever our relationship had become, she was genuinely happy to see me. Her visit was just what I needed to put the whole ugly Hunt business behind me. From here on out, I was sure it was going to be smooth sailing. And I was the king of smooth.

"So, you flew, huh?" I said.

Julianna looked around the airport for a few seconds. I had just enough time to realize what I was saying.

"Uh-huh."

"So, I bet you had to get up early?" I said.

Julianna probably had to force herself not to look at her watch and then at me. She held my glazed look as long as she could. "Imagine how early I would have had to get up if I'd walked," she said.

"You're probably right."

"You haven't changed a bit."

I decided not to think about that comment for too long and said, "You're looking good." It was the understatement of the year. I was realizing just how much I'd missed her.

"So are you," Julianna said, glancing at my eye again. "Skiing, huh?"

"Uh, yeah. Hey, tell me about your job interview. I can't believe you're thinking of moving out here."

"I've interviewed in Kansas City too. And for a job in St. Louis."

"Oh, believe me," I said, "you don't want those jobs."

"I'll take any job right now," she said. "I've got another bag. Let's go get it."

"Sure." We made our way through the crowds toward the luggage pick-up while Julianna filled me in on her itinerary.

"My interview is in Provo. Other than that, I want to play it by ear."

"Who is your interview with?"

"FARMS, at BYU. I may have a couple of other options, but I think that's the job I really want."

I had the sudden image of Julianna in a pair of denim overalls steering a tricycle-wheeled John Deere tractor through a plowed field, her red curly locks bouncing in rhythm with the tractor seat. Wow, even in farm duds she was a magnificent sight.

"I can just see you driving a tractor through a field of alfalfa."

"Cute, Owen."

"I thought your degree was in art history and you had a minor in business. What's with this sudden interest in farming?"

"Not farms, F-A-R-M-S, the Foundation for Ancient Research and Mormon Studies. They don't grow alfalfa."

"What do they grow?"

"Testimonies," Julianna said.

"How do they taste?"

Julianna was playing along. "Sweet."

"Well, I'll have to try one someday." I couldn't help smiling, but the timing just wasn't right.

"So, where can I take you this morning, farm girl?" I was fishing for some clue as to how much time she actually intended to spend with me.

"Oh, I don't know. Where do you want to take me?"

Perfect.

CHAPTER 5

I couldn't think of a better place to take Julianna than to Park City for a little pre-Olympics atmosphere. And it was a beautiful day to boot. We loaded Julianna's luggage in my truck and drove east toward the mountains. Even though it was cold, the sun made a bright appearance, and the snow-covered foothills glistened as it crested the mountain peaks.

"Owen, this is so beautiful. I love it," she said as we drove up the canyon toward Park City proper from Al's place. "Would you ever want to live up here?"

"I don't think I could afford it. Besides, it's too cold."

"I thought it would be a lot colder," she said, turning her face toward the sun. Her light red hair spilled out in curls over her shoulders, perfectly framing her creamy, flawless complexion and bright green eyes. She was unbelievably pretty.

"I think the sun came out today just for you."

Julianna reached out and turned on the radio. I had it tuned to a country station, and she seemed to like it. She was humming along, and then she even started to sing. Her strong, clear voice really surprised me, even though I knew she was talented musically.

"Have you ever considered turning pro?" I asked.

"Turning pro what?"

"Being a professional singer. You have a fantastic voice."

"I don't think the lifestyle would suit me."

"Well, anyway, that's some voice."

"It doesn't compare to yours," Julianna said. "Do you remember that, Owie?" She poked me in the ribs and smiled.

"How could I forget?" She was referring to the time she'd dared me to sing at a karaoke bar in Denver. I'd never really paid her back for that. I was just glad that she and I actually had memories together.

Julianna smiled and kept singing contentedly. I knew I'd never hear that song the same way again.

Before reaching the historic district, I took a sudden turn onto a side street.

"Where are we going?" Julianna asked, turning the music down a little.

"I'm just going to pull into the Buggy Bath and clean this truck off. It shouldn't take more than a minute or two. This thing is filthy."

"You should be ashamed of yourself." Julianna laughed.

I pulled into a three-stall car wash with an industrial vacuum set up just in front of the washing bays. All three bays were in use, but there were no lines, so I pulled into the middle slot to wait.

"Do you mind? It won't take long," I said.

"It's great by me. I just love being up in these mountains."

"I forget that you're a flatlander."

"Still," she said, looking at the tops of the mountains, "I feel at home here too. There's something about these mountains that seems so familiar after seeing them in pictures so often."

"I think so too. Being up here always makes me think about the people who crossed these mountains so many years ago."

"You mean all those pioneer children who walked and walked and walked?" Julianna teased.

"Oh, you're not going to hold that against me forever, are you?"

"Well, the last time we were together, you did use that line in a lame attempt to convince me that you knew all about Mormon history. It was pretty pathetic."

"Guilty as charged," I said. "I suppose now you're going to impress me with your expertise on Summit County lore?"

Julianna scanned the horizon through the windshield. "I'm afraid not. You're the tour guide today."

"They call this Parley's Canyon," I said. "Parley Pratt developed this route for the early Saints. Park City is one of the few cities in Utah that was not originally settled by the LDS people." I was determined to correct my past displays of ignorance and impress Julianna with my historical savvy.

"Hmm? Well, who did settle this area, Owen?" Julianna gave me an innocent look.

I rolled my eyes. Julianna always knew more about everything than I did.

"Go ahead and tell me more," she said. "I shouldn't tease you so mercilessly. You're an awfully nice guy."

"You're not so bad yourself."

There was a long silence where we just looked at each other—awkward, but somehow exhilarating. Julianna ended the silence but not the magic when she turned up the radio and turned on that voice of hers again.

The washing bays on either side of us had cleared, and new cars had filled them. I'd been waiting the longest, but I was sure we'd be next to move forward. After a few more minutes, two cars pulled up to wait on either side of us.

"Do you want to vacuum while we wait?" Julianna asked after her song ended and was replaced by Chalise Porter of KSOP radio promising more music in a minute.

"Sure."

We both got out and shook our floor mats. Julianna picked up a few loose wrappers and examined them. "I'd say, judging strictly from your garbage, that you have an unhealthy emotional attachment to Hostess cupcakes." Julianna held up the empty cellophane evidence and raised an eyebrow.

"Superman had his kryptonite, and I have my cupcakes."

"Well, I'm not going to argue with that. I, myself, have been known to succumb to Almond Roca frenzies."

I put a dollar's worth of tokens in the vacuum slot, and the machine roared to life. I cleaned the driver's side and passed the hose through the cab to Julianna, who did the passenger side. By the time we'd created a tidy environment complete with vacuum marks, several new cars were in line on either side of us.

"This must be the first day of good weather," Julianna said. "Everyone wants a clean car today."

"Look at that. It's a Ford Expedition and a Lexus LS 470 SUV," I said. "And look, behind us—it's a Lincoln Navigator. Further back in line . . ." I craned my neck to look over the seat. ". . . it's a Chevy Tahoe. Only two rigs under forty grand, and I'm sitting in one of them."

"You're right," Julianna said, looking at the expensive cars all around us, "but money can't buy good company."

"A little money might buy you a better tour guide."

"I doubt it. I don't see another tall, dark, and handsome tour guide in the group. I'll stick with you."

My chest tightened and my pulse went up as soon as I heard the words. That was most definitely another flirtatious compliment. I looked away to let my face develop into a full-blown smile and suppressed an urge to shout. I had to change the subject or burst. "Is that rig clean yet?" The vehicle in the bay ahead of us was an older model, red pickup truck—another exception to the forty grand imperative. The man washing it was conservatively dressed in a button-up cowboy shirt and jeans. He waved a bent washing wand back and forth meticulously in one spot and carefully inspected each panel for microscopic dirt particles before moving on. I'd seen him feed the sprayer at least five times since we'd arrived.

"He wants it clean, Owen. Be patient."

"He wants to wear the paint off, that's what he wants. Talk about obsessive."

"Maybe he's got a big date, and he really wants to impress her."

"Should I have washed my truck *before* I picked you up?"

Julianna smiled and shook her head at me.

Another set of cars moved forward into the bays on either side of us as the very particular man with the red pickup in front of us fed yet more coins into his sprayer. "Oh come on, mister, get a move on," I said. "I could have licked your truck clean by now. What is he doing?"

"Don't give him any ideas." There was finally a hint of irritation in Julianna's voice. She was human after all. "It looks like he's spraying the crust and stuff out of his wheel wells."

The lines for the other bays were now three cars deep. It seemed everyone wanted to take advantage of the morning to spiff up the old wagon.

"We're kind of stuck here." I looked around and saw part of a storefront across the street. "That looks like a bookstore across the way. Maybe we should run over and get some reading material. We might be here awhile."

"I didn't know you knew how to read, Owen."

"I don't, but I'm thinking of taking it up. Maybe I should go get a copy of *War and Peace* so I have something to ponder over while this guy does the front end of his truck."

"Be realistic, Owen, you'd only get halfway through the novel by that time."

I might have been seriously aggravated by Mr. Compulsive in front of us if I hadn't been trapped with the woman of the year. I could have stayed in line all winter trading quips. I hoped Julianna felt the same way. My life hadn't offered me a lot of other things to rejoice about lately.

Another set of cars came and went in the neighboring bays while Mr. Clean was still waving the sprayer back and forth, revisiting each square inch of his ride. It was agonizing to watch.

"Look at that poor man next to us," Julianna said, peering over my shoulder.

I looked over and saw a middle-aged man comforting a screaming baby in the front seat of a Chevy Impala.

"Hey, now there's a car I can relate to."

"Not the car, Owen, the baby." Julianna scooted over beside me and leaned on my shoulder to get a better view. She had a worried look on her face. "Oh, she's so tiny."

The infant was very new to this world and apparently very upset about it. I couldn't hear the little thing wail, but it was likely that poor dad was having the earwax blown out of his ears inside that car.

"Look at that little thing go at it," I said.

Julianna looked at me through big, puppy-dog eyes. "She's sad, Owen. That poor man."

"The car ahead of him just got started," I said. "I hope he isn't a relative of the man in front of us. That kid will be grown by the time he gets his front fender clean." I checked out the lines behind us and saw that they were still three cars deep in each lane. Then I looked at my watch. We'd been in line for thirty-five minutes. The man with the very, very clean red truck was getting behind the wheel and looked as though he was about ready to drive away. I thought about picking up a dirt clod and throwing it at his tailgate, but was half afraid he'd indubitably back up and start washing again. I didn't want to be in line when spring arrived.

I looked at the man with the baby and back at Julianna. She was awfully close to me, and it didn't seem like the best time in the world for me to move, but I knew what I had to do.

"Are you thinking what I'm thinking?" she asked.

I nodded and jumped out of the truck to visit the car behind me. The driver was a posh-looking, middle-aged woman in a Mercedes. I tapped on her window, and she rolled it down a couple inches, looking at me with suspicion.

"Excuse me, ma'am. I'm going to let this man next to us swing in ahead of me and go. He has a crying baby and . . ."

She craned her perfectly coifed head closer to the window to see. "Oh sure, do whatever," said the woman. She was reading a magazine and not paying much attention anyway.

I jogged to the front of the new dad's car and motioned for him to slip past me. He nodded and mouthed a thank-you before turning on his engine and making the sharp turn into our lane.

I jumped back into the cab and right into view of Julianna's waiting green eyes. No Boy Scout ever felt so fine after a daily good turn. This was most certainly heaven.

"See, I told you you're a nice guy."

The man with the baby could have taught Mr. Red Truck a lesson on efficient use of car-washing tokens. He waved the sprayer across each section of his car a few times, then off he went, dripping as he drove out of the bay. Julianna and I were spraying the road grime off my truck in no time and back on the road in short order.

We parked a couple of streets off Main and walked toward the city center, passing under a chairlift that began conveniently at the main entrance to a ritzy hotel—the Park City Mountain Resort. There was a line of about twenty skiers, dressed in the latest gear, waiting for the lift. Their smiles gave away the thrill they were experiencing skiing on the same hill as Olympic athletes. I ducked my head as we walked by, hoping that the manager wasn't going to come out and remind me that I was banned from the place for life.

"I remember in the old days having to park and walk to the ski slopes," I said as we passed the lift line.

"The hair-raising ride up the mountain and the excruciating walk to the lodge are part of the experience," Julianna said. "They're missing out."

We turned up Main Street, which amounted to a steep, narrow road of elite shops that mostly sold high-priced art and collectibles. There were more than a few eateries posing as top end restaurants along the street, but definitely no strip-mall establishments.

We walked up the hill, wandered in and out of a few of the art shops, and made small talk about Park City. I tried to remember a few things about the area, but I couldn't come up with much except that the skiing was fantastic. I wanted to say something smarter than that, so I went with the one fact I recalled about Park City. "They used to mine silver up here. In fact, they used to let people tour the mines. The mountains up here are honeycombed with shafts and spurs. It's a wonder the whole place doesn't just cave in."

Julianna laughed and threw back her hair. I couldn't even concentrate on what I was saying.

"So, anyway, is that how the Mormons got so rich?" I wanted to see if she was listening to me.

Julianna gave me a look that said, *I hope you're joking.* I gave back a look that I hoped said, *I'm totally serious.*

"Actually," she began, "Brigham Young discouraged the Saints from . . ." She looked at me again and narrowed her eyes. "Oh, you thought you had me, didn't you? You sneaky devil."

"The Saints did a little logging farther down the hill and up by Heber City," I said, "but other than that, they wisely kept to themselves."

Engaged in more quiet conversation, we passed a few more shops and looked in the windows. "Look! Do you want an Olympic sweatshirt?" I offered.

"Not for sixty bucks." Julianna ignored the shop. She wasn't the type to be extorted. Was this girl perfect or what?

"There's a place I'd like to go." Julianna took my hand and hurried her step.

I tried to see what she was walking toward, but all the shops kind of looked the same to me. I held tightly to her hand and jogged a few steps to catch up.

Julianna turned into a storefront with a sign out front that said "Family Tree." It appeared to be an establishment operated by The Church of Jesus Christ of Latter-day Saints, as the Church's name also appeared on the sign. I wondered what they sold.

The warmth inside the double glass doors was a welcome change from the temperature outside.

"Good morning," said a young woman in a conservative blue sweater and an ankle-length, gray wool skirt. She had long blond hair tied back in a simple ponytail, and she sported a great big smile. A black tag hung on her collar, bearing the name *Sister Kennedy* in small white print. I hoped I wouldn't see the missionaries I was visiting with because then I'd have to fess up, and I wasn't quite ready for that.

"Hi, how are you?" Julianna said, offering the girl her hand.

"Great. I'm Sister Kennedy. Thanks for stopping by."

After a friendly pump of Julianna's arm, Sister Kennedy stuck her hand out in my direction. "Hi," I said, getting one firm shake.

There were several other people milling around the inside of the shop, looking at pictures on the walls. A huge fake tree sprouted up through the floor and branched out over our heads. On the wall immediately inside the doors was a large spreadsheet charting the descendants of a man named Henry Howland, an original Pilgrim. Of interest was that a number of U.S. presidents, including both Bushes, Ford, Nixon, and Roosevelt, were descendents of his family. Joseph Smith and Winston Churchill also shared a lineage with old Henry.

"That's very interesting," Julianna said as she examined each family line.

"You mean you didn't know this already?" I said, mocking her above-average intellect.

Julianna ignored me and spoke to Sister Kennedy. "This is so neat," she said. "I bet it's fun working here."

"Oh, it is," said a very gracious Sister Kennedy.

"So," I said, "are you a relative of the real Kennedy family?"

"My ancestors are as real as it gets," she said as if she'd practiced the comeback before.

"I'll bet you've been asked that a million times," I said.

"No. A million and one now." Sister Kennedy gave me a sly little wink to let me know she was teasing.

Fearing further embarrassment, Julianna took over the conversation. "Is Park City its own mission?"

"It's actually part of the Salt Lake City South Mission. We take turns up here." Now I was getting nervous. I didn't know if the missionaries working with me were in the north or south mission.

I looked around the place while Julianna chatted with Sister Kennedy. There were a few family photos on the wall and a couple of computers set up in viewing areas. People could come in and check their family tree using data from the famous LDS genealogical resources. I turned back to Julianna just in time for her to say something to Sister Kennedy that made me feel like I'd been punched in the stomach.

"I've thought a lot about going on a mission."

I knew enough about LDS missions to realize the serious implications of a comment like that. I wished she hadn't said it so loud. I was afraid a mission president might hear her and whisk her away just when things were going so well between us.

"So, you're members of the Church?" Sister Kennedy asked.

"I am. We're still working on Owen." Julianna gently nudged me in the side.

I opened my mouth to say something, but nothing came out. It was just as well.

"What can you show us in here?" asked Julianna.

"You can access our database," Sister Kennedy said, escorting us dangerously deeper into the room, "or you can watch a few Church commercials on this." She pointed to a computer screen built into a cabinet on the wall. "They're called Mormon Ads. I just love them."

Julianna selected a category of television commercials entitled "Fathers" on the touch-sensitive screen. I'd seen some of the Church-sponsored ads before on television, and I recognized a few. They were clever vignettes around the theme of spending time with your family. Until recently I'd thought they were kind of corny. I suppose that's why I felt so stupid when a tear threatened to roll down my cheek and a sudden warmth flooded my chest. I tried to turn and look away, but Julianna held my hand, keeping me close. She didn't try to disguise her emotions as she watched. She stepped closer to me, and I put my arm around her as the tears rolled freely down her cheeks.

Julianna's open display of emotion was doing nothing to help me hide mine. I was fighting a desperate internal battle with warm fuzzies, and I was losing ground fast. The commercial dads were all prototypes of the dad I never had but definitely the one I wanted to be. Not that my dad was an evil monster; he was just typical of a different era of dad-hood. The McCrays had a dad like those in the ads. That was exactly what I wanted to share with Julianna—I just didn't want to manifest that feeling right there in front of her and the rest of the world in a fit of sobbing. I had my manhood to think about as well as the eternal fate of my soul. I took deep breaths and tried to think about baseball statistics. Julianna was just letting the tears flow.

Sister Kennedy was Johnny-on-the-spot. "Oh, let me see if I have something for you," she said to Julianna, opening a nearby desk. "I think I have a Kleenex here somewhere." She pulled a tissue from within the desk cubby. "Here, you look like you could use this," she said, handing Julianna a powder-blue tissue with little yellow ducks on it.

"Thank you," snuffled Julianna.

Sister Kennedy and Julianna were getting a little too chummy, and I hoped that Julianna wouldn't get really comfortable with the whole mission idea. I would hate to lose her for a year and a half just at this critical time in our relationship.

"Let's go look at the territorial jail museum," I suggested, hoping a tour of a musty underground cell would dry my eyes. "Thank you, Sister Kennedy," I said, guiding Julianna toward the front door.

"You're welcome. And," Sister Kennedy looked at me, "if you'd like, some representatives of the Church could contact you later and talk to you about the Church."

"Oh, no, that's okay. I have friends who could—"

"Nonsense, Owen," said Julianna. "Why don't you talk to the missionaries?"

"Oh, maybe I could call them or something." I feigned indifference.

"I have just the thing," said Sister Kennedy. She searched in a desk drawer and came up empty. "I was going to give you a pass-along card with an eight-hundred number on it, but I think we're out. All these people here for the Olympics have really stressed our supply." Sister Kennedy took a three-by-five card from her backpack and wrote the number on it. "You can take this."

"What is it?" I asked, looking at the card. There was a scripture printed on it.

"That's a Message From Home. I get one every week. They're so I don't get homesick."

"That's so nice," said Julianna.

"You just don't know how important a Message From Home can be once in a while."

"Thanks for the phone number . . . and the card," I added. I thrust the card into the inside breast pocket of my coat without reading it.

"You're welcome. Now, you put that number to some use."

I thought I saw Sister Kennedy wink at Julianna, but I couldn't be sure. She was smooth.

"I'm sure I will," I said.

"Thanks, Sister Kennedy." Julianna rewarded her with a conspiratorial grin.

The first territorial jail was across the street. On the street level was a small replica of a mining tunnel with a few simple mining exhibits. Downstairs was the old jail, which consisted of a couple of cells cut out of the rock. I wondered how much they used the place in the old days and then figured they must have used it quite a bit when Park City was really booming.

We walked around the small room, peering at the walls. It was cold and stark. Julianna noticed some writing on the wall. "Look at this, Owen." She pointed to a place where several prisoners had gouged their names.

I examined the carvings. "I think I arrested that guy," I said.

The museum wasn't very busy, so we lingered a few minutes, admiring the solid rock walls and thick, rusty iron bars.

"I loved those commercials," Julianna said. "Sorry I sobbed like a baby."

I smiled. "Don't worry about it."

"Sister Kennedy sure was nice." She waved a crinkled blue-and-yellow tissue in front of me and then tucked it back in her pocket.

I put my arm around her shoulder and we walked out of the jail, pausing for a few minutes to look at the silver mine exhibit upstairs.

It was getting pretty near noon, and pre-Olympic tourists were starting to crowd the sidewalks. Another storm was brewing, and the wind was picking up. I guessed the temperature must have dropped five degrees since we'd been in Family Tree. As we made our way out onto the street again, Julianna pulled her coat closer around her neck and shivered softly.

"Should we head back to Al's?" I asked. "He wants you to meet Amanda."

"Whatever you say, Owen, my friend," Julianna said, reaching up and taking my hand in hers.

Friend, indeed.

* * *

Amanda took the day off and Al was still on his weekend, so not long after noon we were a foursome enjoying lunch in Al's breakfast nook. Julianna sat in a window seat with the winter sun behind her. Her eyes were incredible. They were the same as her cousin Lewis's, and she reminded me of him.

Al stuck to his nutritional guns and made us low-fat, high-protein, lean beef fajitas on whole-wheat tortillas. Amanda and Julianna, who'd never officially met, were hitting it off. Al was entertaining everyone except me by telling embarrassing police stories *about* me. What a pal.

"So, anyway," Al was saying, "when Owen got to the apartment where the woman with the gun was, he thought he'd been shot. He was all bent over with his hand over his ribs telling everyone it was just a flesh wound and not to worry about him."

Amanda was laughing; she'd obviously heard the story before. Julianna looked terrified.

"You should have seen him. He was the picture of *machismo,*" Al continued. "The trouble was, we'd gotten to the lady before she had a chance to fire a shot, so nobody knew why Owen was bent over bleeding."

"Oh, come on, that's not exactly . . ." I tried to counter.

"Owen," Julianna said, touching me on the arm, "were you really shot?" I got a good whiff of Julianna's perfume when she touched me, and decided I was content to sit there and let Al make a bozo out of me. Normally perfume made me sneeze, but I could inhale *parfum de Julianna* all day long with no negative side effects.

"So," Al went on, "it turns out that when Owen was running down the balcony toward the apartment, he was so focused on getting to the lady with the gun that he didn't see the plywood air conditioner support—minus the air conditioner—hanging out from the window of an adjacent apartment. He ran right into it."

Amanda was still laughing, but Julianna looked unsure of whether to laugh or take pity on me.

"But, Owen," Al said, "where did you go after that? You kind of disappeared. We didn't even have a chance to check out your," he laughed again, "flesh wound."

"I needed a Band-Aid," I said. "And I'm not the only one who does stupid things at work, you know." All heads turned toward me. They were expecting a story. "Just a minute," I said with my finger in the air. "Okay, how about the time when—"

"Oh, man, did I ever tell you about when Owen drove his patrol car off a cliff? Well, he didn't exactly *drive* it off . . ." The official theme of the afternoon seemed to be "Pick On Owen." I'd heard the story plenty of times, so I spent a little quality time looking at Julianna.

Al continued telling the story. "So, when you've got a violator stopped, another cop drives by and you usually give him the code-four signal," he held up four fingers, "just to let him know everything is okay."

Julianna smiled at me and gave me the code four, gracefully waving four of her long, slender fingers at me.

"Now, you have to imagine," said Al, getting to the punch line, "the look on Owen's face when he realized that he'd just waved to his own empty patrol car as it drove by him and off the road. He'd left the thing in drive during the traffic stop." Al was doing the charades version as well, mimicking me waving to my unmanned car. "It rolled forty feet down a cliff before it came to rest upside down."

There was more uncontrollable laughter, and this time, Julianna was laughing nervously while Al and Amanda belly laughed.

"Don't you have to go to bed, Al?" I said.

"Owen, please." Julianna finally loosened up. "I'm enjoying this. It's a side of you I've never seen before. Go on, Al."

"Just a minute," I interrupted, "Al, why don't you tell them about the time you stopped that car and as you approached the window, the car kept lurching forward."

Al glared at me while Amanda and Julianna gave me their complete attention.

"Yeah," I said, "and Al was yelling at the driver, 'Put your foot on the brake! Put your foot on the brake!' When he looked back toward the back of the violator's vehicle, he saw that his empty patrol car was ramming the back of the violator's car."

Amanda looked at Al for confirmation. "That really happened?"

Al smiled and shrugged his shoulders.

"I've got more stories, pal," I threatened.

Al turned to Julianna, who was still laughing. "If you really want to see this stuff up close, you should sign up for a citizen ride while you're here. Then you can see it for yourself—not that this kind of stuff happens every night."

"I'd love that. Is it dangerous?" asked Julianna.

"No, we watch it pretty closely," I said. "You have to ride with a sergeant like Al, who hangs back to supervise. It's pretty safe."

"You should do it, Julianna," Amanda prodded. "I've ridden twice with Al. There are tons of buttons and stuff in the cars. Once after we'd just met, Al was trying to be really cool and turn on his police lights, and the trunk flew up."

"Oh, I've never done that," said Al.

"Yes, you did, remember? You made me jump out and close the trunk."

"Shh!" Al teased.

"There's a good chance that I won't do anything dumb while you're riding, Julianna," I said.

"I'd say the odds are about even," said Al.

"I'll take those odds. When can I go?" asked Julianna.

Al reached for the phone. "Let me just make a call, and I'll fix you up."

Al took the portable phone into the hallway for a few minutes so Amanda and Julianna could continue to torment me. Amanda was telling Julianna about the calls she went on with Al. I was considering becoming a monk.

Al poked his head into the room, the phone still in his ear. "Julianna, are you up for tonight?"

"Sure." Julianna nodded.

Al went back to the hallway and finalized the deal.

"Too bad, Ju," I said. "If you ride with Al tonight, you won't see me at all. I go to work in an hour and get off just when Al goes on."

"That's okay, Owen, I'll miss you, but I'm sure someone will entertain me. You can't be the silliest officer on the force, can you?"

* * *

I didn't have to work hard at keeping busy. Calls for service came in at a steady rate, and that always made the night seem to go faster. Officer-initiated calls were up a little too, simply because the population of Salt Lake's streets was steadily rising as the Games neared. At about ten-thirty, I knew that Julianna would be arriving at the department with Al.

I was feeling pretty good because so far I had managed not to do anything embarrassing that would come up in Al's shift briefing. In fact, I'd made two felony arrests and bagged a guy with an arrest warrant before dinnertime—not a bad take for the night if you threw in a couple of misdemeanor arrests and a traffic ticket.

On my way back to the station, I received one of those last-minute calls.

"Salt Lake to David twenty-one," the dispatcher broadcasted my call sign. David was the downtown designation, and twenty-one was my call number.

"David twenty-one, go ahead," I said into a microphone.

"Respond to a disturbance in progress at 242 South 700 East, McDonald's Drive-in."

"Go ahead with the details," I said.

"David twenty-one," said the dispatcher. "Two suspects: number one, a white male, six-foot, brown hair and goatee, wearing jeans and dark jacket. Number two . . ."

"Go ahead."

"A white male, over six foot, wearing jeans and red checkered flannel shirt and vest. Subjects are intoxicated and disorderly, threatening a passerby. Manager at McDonald's would like contact."

"Copy. I'm en route." I stepped up my speed a little, choosing not to run with my lights. I usually made it to a call just as fast going about the speed limit as I did trying to hurry with my overheads on. Citizen drivers made some of the most stupendous maneuvers when they saw a police car running up behind them with its emergency lights on.

It was a short run to McDonald's, and I thought maybe with a little luck I could solve the problem just by showing up. I was getting nearer when I heard a familiar voice check into service on the radio.

"Salt Lake, David thirty-one, in service. I'll back up David twenty-one." That was Al, and he was checking into service from the station to cover me. It was just before the start of his shift, but I knew he was checking in early to see that Julianna and I saw each other tonight.

"Copy, David thirty-one, covering David twenty-one," said the dispatcher's voice on the radio.

"I'm just about there, thirty-one," I told Al over the radio.

"Why don't you come from the north."

"Copy." Al's voice was fresh and crisp over the radio. "Also, I have your x-ray with me."

That was radio language telling me that Julianna was aboard. The code x-ray was usually reserved for wives; Al couldn't resist a chance to needle me over the radio.

"David twenty-one," I told the dispatcher, "show me out in the parking lot at McDonald's."

"Copy, David twenty-one is out in the parking lot," he confirmed.

I pulled into a parking lot across the street and watched as two goofy-looking rednecks taunted a small Asian man who was walking down the sidewalk with a bag of groceries in each arm.

I couldn't hear what was being said, but the context of the situation was obvious from the antics of the two trouble-makers. They were dancing around the man, making kick-boxing gestures and laughing. They were both holding to-go bags from McDonald's and large paper cups. A small crowd of onlookers peered from the McDonald's entry, waiting for something to happen.

The little man made several attempts to ignore the buffoons and walk around them, but they kept lumbering into his path, once nearly making him drop his groceries.

Al pulled up across the street from the north side of the lot, as directed, and opened his car door. I could see the shadowy shape of someone in the passenger seat.

I was about halfway across the street, walking toward the two men, when something completely unexpected happened. The small Asian man stopped and faced the two drunks, bowing slightly in their direction. With a movement as fast as lightning, the man's feet went into action. All I really saw was the air filled with two all-beef patties, special sauce, lettuce, cheese, pickles, onions, and sesame seed buns. French fries skittered all over the parking lot, and the contents of two cups of pop and ice sparkled in the phosphorous lights and rained down on the two misfits. The little man had touched neither of them. There was nothing left of their McDonald's meals but the tops of their shredded paper bags clenched tightly in their grubby, fat fists. They stood motionless with their mouths half-open, looking at the remains of the supersized meals strewn over the blacktop.

I looked at Al for a reaction; we were both trying to keep straight faces. I intervened before Ditz and Dutz decided to do something that would really make the little man mad.

"Hold on there, fellas," I said striding, toward them.

"Did you see what he just did?" asked the tall one in the red plaid shirt and down vest. He looked at me like I was going to scold the Asian gentleman, who was standing on the sidewalk, grocery bags still in his arms.

"Yes, sir, I did."

"Well, he's gonna have to pay for this," he said, pointing to his dinner.

The little man simply bowed to me, apparently willing to do whatever I asked.

"Gee," I said, rubbing my chin and then pointing to the grocery bags the little man was carrying, "those grocery bags look awfully heavy. I could ask him to set those down so we can talk this out. But, golly, there's no telling what he might do to you with his hands free." I tapped my finger on my chin. "Or, maybe you guys could call this a loss and make yourselves disappear."

The two men looked at each other with dumb expressions. They looked like the type that had a very small repertoire of expressions to choose from.

"Sir," I said to the little man, "are those heavy?"

He shook his head and bowed again. "I pay for meals," he said softly.

"No, no. I don't think you will."

"What's it going to be gentlemen? I'd hate to see just what he can spill across the parking lot with his hands free."

"Alright," said the kid with the goatee. "We're leaving."

"Good choice. Now, before you do that, let's have a look at your driver's licenses."

I took their names and checked them for outstanding warrants before letting them go. The manager at McDonald's was thankful, as was the little man, who bowed at me seven hundred times before finally continuing down the street.

By the time I was done getting everyone's name for my report, Al and Julianna were both standing in the parking lot with me.

"Good work, Officer Richards. Nice to see my tax dollars at work," said Julianna.

"Since when do you pay taxes in Salt Lake City?" I asked.

"Since Amanda and I are going shopping tomorrow."

"I guess you got me there." I replaced the little notebook of names in my breast pocket. "And you," I shook an accusing finger at Al, "you almost had me laughing so hard I couldn't talk to those guys."

"Like I could help it. Did you see those fries go up? It looked like Mount Vesuvius."

We enjoyed a good laugh, mostly out of the earshot of the public until three young men dressed in fraternity sweatshirts exited the McDonald's.

"Well, if it isn't the jackboot brigade," said one of the boys, holding the door open for his partners.

Al and I stopped and looked. "Do you think he means us?" Al asked just loud enough for the three boys to hear.

"Yes, you," said another one. "You guys got your Nazi boots on?"

"Fascists," spat the third boy.

Julianna looked surprised.

I didn't say anything to her, but she got the drift. This was just one of the many perks of being a police officer. Some people love you, and some don't.

"Look at that," said the first young man. "Guns and nightsticks. Are you going to beat me, police man?"

"Communist pigs." The second boy was walking closer to see if he could get a response.

Al said, just loud enough to be heard by the boys, "First fascists, now communists? Which side of the political spectrum are they accusing us of being on?"

The closest boy heard Al and changed the subject to something he knew about. "What's the matter, piggy? Can't think of anything to arrest me for?"

"You guys are nothing but the embodiment of a tyrannical Marxist regime," said the first young man, obviously proud of his first semester of Philosophy 101 at the U. He was coming dangerously close to us, and there was a fire in his eye. I'd been a cop long enough to know that sometimes very ugly things could happen in an instant.

I stepped back with my right foot, leaving my left foot slightly ahead and bearing very little weight. If this kid wanted to get any closer, he'd have to come through a beastly left snap kick.

Al moved to approach the kid as well, but I warned him off with a signal behind my back. I placed my four fingers on my leg just under my holster, out of the view of the kid. Al glanced down and backed off. I just didn't want to make a big scene. Al understood as if he'd read my thoughts. He stepped back and kept the other two guys in sight.

"Come on, hit me, cop. Hit me." The first boy was coming closer still, turning his back to me and egging me on.

"Well, what are you waiting for, pig?" he asked.

I let out a long sigh, called up my best Ivy League accent, and said, "I'm waiting for a sentence with the word *bourgeoisie* in it."

The boy looked at me in wonder and then at his friends. It was a standoff, and I think the boys realized we'd won the intellectual part of the contest. After a brief pause, the angry spark in their eyes dimmed and they turned to leave.

"It's French. Look it up." I couldn't resist a parting shot, but I used my nicest tone of voice. The three boys walked silently to their car and got in. We watched them drive away before I burst out laughing.

Julianna was amused but taken aback. "Is it like this every night?" she asked.

"Every night," I said. "Never a dull moment."

"So was that the little signal you were talking about? The code four?"

"Yessiree bobcat tail," I said.

"It seemed to work."

"It usually does," I said. "By the way, was that right?"

"Was what right?" asked Julianna.

"Bourgeoisie."

"Perfect," she said.

"Good, I'm a little rusty on my . . . Marxist theory, or whatever that boy was spewing."

"Don't worry, your French was just perfect. It'll take those guys at least a week to figure out how to spell it so they can look it up."

We shared a good laugh before Al was dispatched to something else. I was a little disappointed that Julianna had to leave with Al because of the department policy requiring citizen riders to go with supervisors. I would have liked to have driven her home.

Satisfied that the night was over for me, I said my good-byes and got back in my car. I knew Julianna was going to have a good time with Al.

I was already on thirty minutes of overtime, so I drove directly to the department. As I pulled my patrol car into the chain-linked parking area, I saw the outline of a man leaning up against the parking structure smoking. Not many of our officers smoked, so I took a second look.

The man wore a waist-length jacket and had a hat pulled low over his eyes. As I passed him, he blew a thick funnel of smoke in my direction, which masked any features I might have been able to make out.

I'd just passed the parking structure when the man flipped his hat off and walked toward my car from the rear, peering at me in my rearview mirror. It was Raymond Hunt.

My first reaction was to dynamite the brakes. Hunt threw down the cigarette, laughed, and ran away from me into the parking garage, where he disappeared from view. I couldn't see him from the car, so I bailed out. Once on foot, I ran to the entrance of the structure and stopped, listening for his footsteps. I reached for my lapel microphone and requested backup.

"David twenty-one in foot pursuit at the back lot," I told the dispatch center.

"Copy, David twenty-one in foot pursuit. Your location, twenty-one?"

"Back lot," I said. "Back lot of the PD."

Before the dispatcher could request backup for me, other units started to check in on the radio. Most of the officers were responding from the station, either having just finished their shift or just come on. No one wanted to miss the excitement.

I still couldn't see Hunt, so I simply directed the responding units to form a perimeter around the police department.

"All responding units," I said while running, "let's try to get a five-block perimeter around the station." Five blocks might have seemed excessive, but when you considered how far a person could run in just a few minutes, five blocks may have been too small a perimeter. Besides, a good tactician could always shrink a perimeter, but it never did much good to enlarge one after the prey had escaped.

There had been a lot of radio traffic while the officers took positions around the department. What followed was a natural lull while everyone waited for more information. The dispatcher, anxious to feed us more details, took advantage of the dead radio air.

"David twenty-one, your status?"

"I'm code four," I answered, letting him know I was not in immediate danger.

"Suspect information?" the dispatcher asked.

"A white male, dark jacket and hat, medium build. He's on foot, last seen in the parking structure. I no longer have contact with him." And, as an afterthought, I said, "Consider the suspect armed; it was Raymond Hunt."

Raymond Hunt was a name familiar to every officer in the department; you didn't shoot a cop and not create a memorable reputation.

I saw police cars driving every direction around the department, trying to establish some kind of containment from which the suspect couldn't escape. Al, who was the sergeant in charge of the graveyard shift, was giving most of the commands over the radio. He eventually got a command post set up outside the perimeter and asked me by radio if I could contact him in person.

He had organized a small group of his officers to try to contain anyone who was still in the structure and had established a broader visual perimeter of about a three-block circumference so that Hunt couldn't leave the area without being seen.

I was out of breath by the time I reached Al several blocks away, mostly from the anxiety I felt at having seen Hunt so clearly.

The command center wasn't a converted recreational vehicle with antennas all over the hood, it was just Al standing by his car with a radio mic in his hand. Julianna was there too.

"How are you, Owen?" was his first question. Not "Where did you see Hunt last?" or "Which direction was he headed?" Al wanted to know how I was. That wasn't necessarily a good sign.

"I'm fine," I said, catching my breath. "I don't know where he went."

Julianna stepped back, and Al came a little closer. "What did you see, Owen?"

"He was standing at the back of the PD lot near the parking structure," I said quickly. "He was looking down with the top of his face covered by his hat. He waited until I was too far into the lot to get back quickly, and then he made sure I saw him." I could see the disbelief growing in Al's eyes. "I know it was him, Al. No mistake."

I think he wanted to ask me if I was this certain on the ski slope, but he didn't. Instead he did what any good friend and good supervisor would do.

"We're holding swing shift over to help with the perimeter," he told me. "The rest of us will scour this place. If he went to ground anywhere inside the perimeter, we'll get him." Al put his hand on my shoulder.

"He threw a cigarette butt," I said. "We can have that tested."

Al nodded.

Somewhere in my gut I knew we weren't going to find Hunt inside our net. Al knew it too—I could tell by the look on his face. He was fighting with the same doubts I was, and the doubts were winning. I felt like a fool.

Julianna had a worried look on her face. I hoped she wasn't thinking the same thing the rest of the officers were: Owen has cracked.

CHAPTER 6

After two hours of searching we'd found no sign of Hunt, and Al relieved all the swing shift officers from duty. When I came out of the locker room, Julianna was sitting alone in the break room at a table.

"How's the ride been so far?" I asked.

"Not what I expected."

"Where's Al?" I wanted to make sure the coast was clear before I talked to Julianna.

"He's on the phone. He told me to wait here."

"So, what did you expect tonight?"

"Oh, I don't know. Not *this.*"

I wasn't sure what she meant by *this*, but I decided not to take it personally. "It hasn't been my best night," I said. "About half the department is convinced that there is no way Hunt could be alive. They probably think I'm crazy."

"What does the other half think?" she asked.

"The other half is sure I'm crazy." I laughed a little to break the tension.

Julianna didn't look sure if she should laugh with me or not. "Don't be so hard on yourself," she said, looking at me sympathetically.

"If you and Amanda are shopping tomorrow, you're going to be one tired little redhead."

"I know, but I need to go. Amanda's taking the morning off to go with me. We're going to look for something sophisticated for me to wear to my interview. She's so nice. She and Al really make a great couple." Julianna was twirling a lock of her hair around her finger.

I nodded. I liked Amanda too, but the conversation smacked of seriousness, so I tried another tactic. "So, what interview do you have? This isn't the farming thing, is it?"

"It's F-A-R-M-S, and yes it is."

"And you're out and about at . . ." I looked at my watch, "two in the morning?"

Julianna looked sheepish. "I wanted to see where you worked," she said. "Besides, I have almost no chance at this job. I was lucky to get an interview."

"Oh, come on now. I'd hire you."

"You still think this is an alfalfa-farmer job."

"True. Big acronyms scare me, especially this FARMS thing—Foundation for Agricultural Research on Mormon Alfalfa Plantings something . . . something."

"That was almost it." Julianna laughed. "Anyway, I am a very efficient shopper, and I can sleep in tomorrow. I don't have to pick up my rental car until one in the afternoon."

"I wish you didn't have to spend money on a rental."

"It's okay; I've been saving up. I knew I'd have to rent something. I'll just have Amanda drop me at the car rental lot. I should have plenty of time to get to Provo for my four-thirty interview. After that I thought I'd spend some time with Great-aunt Etta in Lindon."

"Aunt Etta? Now there's one of my favorite people in the whole world. What's she doing in Lindon? I thought she lived in Ephraim."

"Not anymore. She sold her place and moved to Lindon. She's taking classes at BYU now."

"Classes? Classes in what? Gerontology? She has to be pushing ninety."

"I think she's taking a bunch of classes just for fun. She can afford to be a little eclectic at her age."

"I'll say. In fact, she's more than electric—she's on fire."

"I said *eclectic,*" Julianna corrected.

I smiled at her, and she smiled back.

It had been a long night for both of us. I wanted to get away from the department, and I knew that Julianna really wanted to get home and get to bed.

"Al's going to be tied up for a while," I said.

"I know. He was on the phone with your lieutenant before I came in here."

"That's never a good sign." I got the feeling that Julianna had picked up on the fact that this situation was not looking good for me.

"Al told me a little bit about this. He's really sticking up for you."

I had no idea how much she knew, but it didn't matter.

"He always has," I said. "He's always there when someone needs him. Can I drop you off somewhere?"

"Sure." Julianna sensed that I didn't want to talk.

We walked past Al's office and saw that he was on the phone. I gestured to him that I was going to drive her home, and he nodded, then covered the phone with one hand and said to Julianna, "Thanks for coming along."

"Thanks, Al. I'm sure I'll see you around." She waved and we left the department.

We walked out past the parking structure to my truck. I was wary of Hunt, still convinced that he was somewhere around. There was a thick frost on the window, so I spent a few minutes scraping ice and warming things up while Julianna got comfortable in the passenger seat.

After we got on the road, she turned to look at me. "What?" I asked as she stared.

"Al told me that you're a good cop," she said, but she didn't elaborate.

"Well, Al is a nice guy."

"He didn't say it to be nice," she said. "He said it because he's worried."

"Did he tell you he was worried?"

"No, but you guys are good friends, and I can tell that he's upset about this whole thing."

I was a little uncomfortable accepting vicarious praise. "Al's a good cop too," I said.

"He wasn't telling me that so I could stroke your ego. He's worried about what some people might be thinking."

"I know what they're thinking."

"But Al trusts you. He trusts your instincts."

I didn't say anything. What could I say? Of all the conversations that I could have been having with Julianna, this one was dead last on my wish list. I really liked this girl, and now I'd wrapped her up in this confusing mess.

"Owen," Julianna said.

I looked over at her soft features in the rhythmic glow of the passing streetlights. "Yeah?"

"Al didn't tell me to tell you that. I think he just wants me to trust you . . . the same way he trusts you." She reached over and touched my face where my bruised eye was going from blue to green. "I do."

* * *

After I dropped Julianna off at her friend's place on Fort Union Boulevard, I went back to my condo for a bite to eat and to try to sleep off the fatigue and embarrassment of the night. The place smelled stale even though it hadn't been vacant for long. The food in the refrigerator looked like the remains of a failed chemistry experiment and completely ruined my appetite.

I tried unsuccessfully to sleep, wondering, as I stared at the ceiling, what kind of knot head I'd made of myself. As the night wore on, I became more and more convinced that I hadn't seen Hunt at all. The only other reasonable explanation was that I was cracking up. I tossed that idea around for the rest of the night as the sandman mocked me from the inside of my eyelids.

Things looked a little better in the morning, not because anything had changed, but because it was morning and that's just how things work. I was glad for small miracles.

The phone rang while I was in the shower, and I had to jump out and answer it wrapped in a towel.

"Hello?" I said into the receiver.

It was the voice of the administrative secretary at the PD. I'd come to know her recently through the process of applying for an assignment to the detective's office. She was one of those salt-of-the-earth types, full of encouragement and joy. She was also privy to all that went on in the department, good and bad. This morning her tone was tight and uncomfortable. She told me that I had a 9:00 A.M. meeting with the patrol lieutenant, but didn't tell me what the meeting was about. I didn't have to ask, and I'm sure she was glad I didn't.

I hung up the phone and wandered back into the shower to rinse the shampoo out of my hair. Sometimes it didn't pay to answer the phone.

The Salt Lake City Police Department was housed in a downtown building that was old, austere, and minimally functional. As I entered the building, I pushed my doubts about seeing Hunt out of my head—to the extent that I could.

Several other officers were milling about, absorbed in their tasks. No one looked up as I walked by. I understood the reason. I went straight to Lieutenant Michaels's office for the bad news.

"Thanks for coming in, Owen," he said from behind a neatly organized desk. He was young for his rank, but well qualified and experienced. He was tall and thin, with a full head of sandy-brown hair just starting to turn gray at the temples.

"No problem," I said, wondering why Lieutenant Michaels was treating my visit like it had been optional.

"Would you swing the door shut, please?"

"Sure." I pushed the door closed slowly to give me time to think about what dreaded news I was about to receive.

On the desk in front of the lieutenant was a short stack of papers. He ran his finger down the side of the stack and fanned the corner. His face gave away very little, except that the way he stared intently at the papers told me that he was as uncomfortable as I was.

"You've had a rough week," he said. "Are you doing okay?"

This was not how I wanted to start a conversation with the lieutenant. My mind went back to my experiences with the department psychologist after Lewis's death. It was always, "Are you okay? What would you like to talk about? Can we work through this?" No one ever offered to chalk up my strange experience in Missouri to one of life's little oddities and move on. No, this wasn't how I wanted this conversation to start. Was I okay? I was beginning to wonder.

"Yes," I said. I could have elaborated, but that would have just gotten me into more trouble.

"I'm going to put you on light duty, Owen. I'm sorry," he said before I had a chance to object. His bluntness hurt, but I think he was just trying to make it quick.

Light duty was the equivalent of being on the practice squad in Little League football. You were still on the team, but you didn't get to play. Officers on light duty filed reports and answered phones. If you broke your leg playing softball in the park, light duty was okay. If you found yourself on light duty because you made your whole department chase the imaginary shadow of the man who killed your best friend, then you might as well wear a Tupperware ring mold on your head because everyone thinks your brain has turned to Jell-O.

I was silent for a moment, thinking about the best way to respond. A tantrum would simply reassure the command staff that they'd made the right choice in taking a precaution with me. Sulking would probably get me another free ride on the psychologist's couch. As it was, I didn't have to say anything because my silence must have spoken volumes.

"I know this is very upsetting, Owen." Lieutenant Michaels pushed the pile of papers to the side of his desk and leaned forward. "We've been pulling our hair out all morning over this. In the end, we just had to play the odds."

"What do you mean 'play the odds'?" I wanted to say more, but I bit my lip.

"I have to be straight with you, Owen. We don't know what to believe about all this."

"And," I said to save him the trouble, "it's a safer bet to keep me off the streets. Is that it?"

The lieutenant looked at me for a moment and then slowly nodded his head.

If I thought it was going to help my case I might have come up with a better argument. As it was, I felt a tantrum coming on, but I knew that would do more harm than good. I cut my losses and told Michaels I would take a day or two off.

"It's not a day or two I'm asking for, Owen," he said. "It's until the Olympics are over."

"What?" I burst out of my chair. "That's nearly a month! And at a time when you can't afford to lose anybody. You've got to be kidding!"

"I'm sorry, Owen." Lieutenant Michaels rose from his seat and came around his desk. "I don't know if this is the best thing to do, but it seems to be the safest."

I took a deep breath and let it out, staring into his eyes. I couldn't begin to describe the emotions running through me. Well, maybe I could, but not in polite company. Lieutenant Michaels set his jaw, and I could read in his eyes that the die was cast. I wasn't going to work the 2002 Olympics.

I simmered down and gave in peacefully, hoping to score a few sanity points by not blowing my lid. "So, other than running errands for the records clerk," I said, a little too sarcastically, "what am I supposed to do?"

"Well, we thought you could use the time to—"

"Just tell me how many days a week I have to sit on the big leather couch with the department psychologist."

"That's not up to me. Your first visit is next week. Monday," he said, looking at his watch. "We'll see after that."

"As long as I make my appointments with the shrink, is there any reason why I can't take some time off instead of ride the front desk?"

"If you have enough vacation built up, I'll approve the time off. That might be better than being here."

"I have the time. I'll turn in the paperwork. Is that all?" I said, turning my back to Michaels and facing the door like a spoiled child.

"Owen," Lieutenant Michaels urged, "please help us out on this. We've got to look at the big picture. You're going to be with us for a long time, and the next few weeks could be pivotal—not just for Salt Lake, but for you as well."

"Yeah, thanks." I wasn't very sincere, but the lieutenant could see I was stinging, and he understood the hint of attitude in my voice.

"If it makes you feel any better, Owen, a lot of us reach a point in our lives when we have to make some emotional adjustments. I've been there. So have a lot of guys."

I thought about that for a few seconds. "I don't know. It's been a tough week for me." I would have said almost anything to get out of his office.

"You just keep your chin up, Owen. You've always been a straight shooter." The lieutenant's understanding was touching, but I was in no mood. I opened the door and left his office without another word.

Now that I was a temporary member of real society, I had to think about what day it was according to the world. It was my Tuesday, so that made it . . . Friday. Al would be sleeping off his night shift, and Julianna would be busy all day. I was feeling a little lost. I wondered what Elder Rose and Elder Cannon were doing and gave that some thought as I drove to my condo.

I was sitting on my couch watching a rerun of *I Love Lucy* and thinking about Al and Amanda's fairy-tale life when someone knocked on the door. I opened it to find my two favorite elders wearing their black trench coats.

"Elders, I was just thinking about you two."

They exchanged looks.

"Hello, Owen. How is . . . everything?" Elder Rose still did most of the talking. He landed so hard on the word *everything* that I thought maybe he knew about the meeting I had just had.

"Fine." I shook their hands and gestured for them to come inside.

"We can't stay long. We just felt like we should drop by."

"I'm glad you did."

"We kind of wondered if you'd given any thought to a baptism date."

"Oh, the date. I've thought about it."

"Great! Can we schedule it?"

"Not quite yet," I said. "There's still one person I need to talk to."

"I have an idea," Elder Rose said. "Why don't you just pick a date and see what happens? I have a feeling that if you take the first step, the Lord will take care of the rest."

"I have a friend who lives out of state, and I'd really like her to be there. I have to check the date with her."

"Trust us on this, Owen."

I'd stalled long enough. I knew that when Julianna found out about my baptism, she'd move heaven and earth to be there. "Okay, you win. Let's try for—"

"No, you have to write it down."

"Write it down?"

"Yes, I think it's important."

Elder Rose held out a pen. I looked for a scrap of paper and then remembered the card that Sister Kennedy had given me. I found it in my coat pocket and took the pen offered by Elder Rose.

"Hey," said Elder Cannon, the silent one, "where did you get that?"

"The card?" It was a pretty normal card except for the scripture written on it. I hadn't seen it before, but someone had colored a flower on one side. "Oh, I got this from one of your cohorts in Park City."

"Sister Kennedy?" asked Cannon.

"How'd you know?"

"Everyone knows about her famous Messages From Home. She's a walking billboard for missionary support."

Elder Rose was nodding. Apparently Sister Kennedy was a minor folk hero.

"Yeah, I remember. She said it was a Message From Home."

I acted like I was going to write something and then said, "Hey, guys, there's just one more thing I have to do before I can nail down a date."

The elders looked at each other with disappointment.

"Really guys," I said, "I'll keep the card with me and the next time you see me, there will be a date written on it. I promise."

"Sounds good," Elder Rose said, even though I could tell it didn't sound that good to him. "Until next time."

"Until next time," I said, feeling as though I'd let these two men down. I felt a little down myself.

We shook hands and they left. I looked out the window to see if they got into a car, but I didn't see one.

I flipped the card in my fingers for a few minutes but still didn't read the scripture. My mind was elsewhere. I put the card back in my coat pocket.

I thought about Julianna shopping her little heart out and renting a car to drive south to her interview. If I could find her, I could take her to Provo myself. It was only eleven-thirty. Maybe I could make something of the day after all.

Now, I thought, *where does a woman from Kansas City go to buy clothes for a big interview?* How was I supposed to know? I did all my clothes shopping at Wal-Mart—once a year.

There was really only one solution. Every good cop knows how to make use of confidential informants. I picked up the phone and called the girl who cut my hair.

"Hello, Salon N.V.," said a female voice.

"Hello, is Belle there?"

"She's with a client," said the voice. "Can I take your number and have her call you?"

"It's really, really important," I said.

The voice turned irritated. "Just a minute."

A few minutes ticked off the clock while I waited on hold, listening to pop music that prevented me from generating any productive thought.

When the phone finally clicked on, I heard the familiar voice of Belle. "Hello, this is Belle."

"Belle, this is Owen Richards."

There was a few seconds of silence. "Owen Richards. Second Tuesday of every month whether you need it or not? That Owen Richards?"

"Yes, I have a big favor to ask."

"Sure, I just finished with a client. Shoot."

Belle was the only person I knew who was connected to the world of style and fashion. If anybody could tell me where a city girl like Julianna would look for interview clothes, Belle could. From her bizarre choices in hair colors to her groovy pants, she was always sporting the latest style.

"Belle, I need to find someone."

"I hope I can help." She sounded a little dubious.

"She's shopping right now."

"Oh." Now she sounded confident, as if she were in her element. "And you want me to tell you where she is?"

"Exactly."

"I need some information to go off. Tell me what you know."

"Okay, she has an interview this afternoon, and she's looking for something to wear to it."

"Kind of job?" asked Belle.

"Uh . . ." She had to ask, didn't she? "Something like farming."

"Farming?" Belle said.

"No, like some ancient research study place for Mormons." Why didn't I pay more attention to details?

"Got it. What does she dress like?"

"I don't know. What do you mean?"

"Is she trendy or old-fashioned?"

"Oh, fashionable, but not too trendy."

"Flashy or understated?"

"More understated, I think."

"Thrifty or reckless with money?"

"Thrifty."

"Madonna or school marm?"

"More school marm."

"Okay, Meier and Frank."

"She's pretty frank."

"No, Owen, not 'is she frank?' Meier and Frank—the department store. My heavens."

"Belle, you're a peach. Next haircut, there's a big tip in it for you if I find her."

"Start at the ZCMI Center and work your way south. You'll find her."

I hung up and headed directly out the door, stopping briefly to brush my teeth and tame my hair with a few handfuls of water. Then I charged out to my truck.

I was at the ZCMI Center and in the front doors of Meier and Frank just after noon. I hoped I hadn't missed the girls, but wondered how hard it could be to find two of the most beautiful women on earth in one department store.

I spent the next hour lost in Meier and Frank. The only landmark I could keep track of was the perfume counter because every time I came close, I sneezed and my eyes watered.

I had no idea how women's clothing stores kept track of their wares. There was a section for teens and for young teens;

there was a section for mature styles (whatever those were) and for sporty styles; there was a section for girls' clothes and one for infants; there was a section for petite women and for pregnant women. I had to walk between the crowded racks, risking being attacked by pantsuits and dresses. Each time I knocked something off its hanger, it took me fifteen minutes to get it back on the hanger and on the rack. Every episode added to my already overdeveloped hatred for shopping. At the rate I was going, Julianna would make it to her interview, get the job, and retire before I found her.

Desperate times called for desperate measures, so I asked the perfume girl (who must have had some alien immunity to respiratory irritation) where I could find the information center. She directed me to the back of the store, and I looked around, trying to find something that looked like a back of the store. Finally she pointed it out, and I made it to a back reception area labeled, appropriately, "Customer Service."

"I've lost my wife," I lied. "Is there some way to page her?"

The receptionist smiled and nodded. She picked up her telephone and asked me what my name was.

"Owen. My wife's name is Julianna, and Amanda."

The receptionist stopped, the phone halfway to her ear.

"I mean, her name is Julianna; my daughter's name is Amanda."

The smile returned, and the receptionist proceeded to make the most embarrassing page in the history of Meier and Frank.

"Would Julianna and little Amanda please dial zero from any register phone. Your daddy has been found."

I put my hands over my face and slumped into a nearby chair. Couldn't anything go my way? Nothing happened for about five minutes, so I sneaked out of the back room. The receptionist gave me a shrug as I left.

It was two-thirty. I figured they'd be long gone by then, so I walked slowly through the store, unsure if I was headed to the outside doors or not—not that it mattered. I was just focused on moping when I heard a familiar giggle. It was Julianna.

I ducked behind a rack of ladies' sweaters and peeked through the middle. Julianna and Amanda were talking and laughing, their arms full of store bags. I circled them until I was behind them, then walked quietly in their direction. When I was directly behind Julianna, I spoke in a Deep South sheriff's voice.

"Ma'am, I'll have to see the receipts for them there clothes."

Julianna swung around, eyes wide, and gasped when she saw me. "Owen Richards, you scared the tar out of me! What are you doing here?"

"I just happened to have some spare time, so I thought I'd do some shopping."

"In the women's section?" asked Amanda.

I hadn't noticed, but I was standing between a rack of long gowns and a rounder of women's shirts that were probably more accurately called *blouses.*

"I have an outfit that would go great with one of these," I said, draping the end of a gown over my arm.

"I'll bet you do. What else haven't you told us?" Julianna took the dress from my arm and let it fall back into place on the rack. "So, I thought you had to work."

"I had an unscheduled vacation day to take."

"So you came to see us?"

"What better way to spend a vacation day?" I said.

"I'm glad you're here, Owen. Can I ask you a favor?"

"Anything."

"We kind of lost track of time. Do you think you could run me out to the airport so Amanda can get back to work?"

"That's a good idea," said Amanda. "I have to get back, or who knows what kind of mess I'll find."

"I'm sorry," I said, "but I can't take you to the airport."

"Oh," said Julianna.

"I can take you to Provo, though."

"Oh, you can't do that, Owen. Let me just rent a car."

"Nonsense," I said, and it was settled. Amanda was glad to be able to run back to work, and Julianna was glad not to spend her savings on a rental car. This wasn't working out half bad.

"Owen," said Julianna just after we parted ways with Amanda, "did you have us paged?"

"Did I have you paged?" I said in a minor panic. There was no recovery for my attempt to buy time. The gig was up. I dropped my shoulders in a defeated slump.

"You did." Julianna tipped her head back and let out a roar. "Wait until I tell Amanda. We both thought there was something fishy about that, 'We found your daddy.' Oh, that's precious. I should have known it was you."

Julianna continued to laugh while I wondered why on earth everything lame should be attributed automatically to me.

Our trip south went well, meaning that I didn't embarrass myself further. A song I knew came on the radio, and I sang along, a rarity for me.

"Wow, Owen—you really can sing. I had no idea. The last time I heard you sing, well . . ."

"The last time," I said, narrowing my eyes, "I was duped. I'll get you back."

"I'm quaking in my boots."

The drive to Provo wasn't very long, but even so, it seemed to go by too fast.

"I hate for you to have to wait around for me while I'm at the interview," she said.

"Why don't you just take the truck and drop me off at your Aunt Etta's," I suggested. "She and I have some catching up to do."

"If you don't mind."

"No, of course not. I love Aunt Etta."

"I meant me taking your truck."

"Anything for you." She had no idea how much I meant it.

We pulled up in front of Etta's new house in time for Julianna to run inside, say a flying hello to Etta, change into her new skirt and blazer, freshen up, and run back out to the truck.

I found myself alone with Etta and someone new to me—her little Chihuahua mix, Sparky. Sparky was about the size of a loaf of bread, with red and white hair. He looked like he'd been a handful in his day. His eyes were glassy now, and he didn't make much noise when we arrived. I gave him a quick scratch under the neck, and he stuck with me like glue.

"Don't worry about Sparky," Etta said. "He's deaf and mostly blind. I inherited him from his old master, who passed away."

Etta lived in a smart little spec house, white with light gray trim and fake shutters on the windows. It was a cracker box compared to her old house in Ephraim. The front door to her new home was steel with a small peephole, nothing like the huge oak door with the leaded glass oval that I remembered. It was through that wavy glass that I'd first seen Julianna, and I remembered the scene fondly.

Etta was the same vigorous old woman I'd always known, but the surroundings didn't seem to fit her. The small living room was decorated with new furniture, and the place smelled like fresh paint, not hot pastries. There was a wicker basket on the floor that contained all manner of toddler toys. As I walked past it, my pant cuff caught on the basket and the contents spilled out on the floor.

"Oh, I'm so sorry about that. I meant to have that basket put away before you kids got here," Etta said. She bent over and started throwing toys back in the basket. "They're for the grandkids. Grammy's toys."

"Here, let me get them." I picked up toys at warp speed so that Etta didn't have to. She was spry for her age, but she didn't need to push it. I stowed them in the closet, and Etta waved me into the kitchen, where she was most comfortable.

"So, Owen," she said, but she didn't continue.

"So, what?"

"So, are you two getting along fabulously?"

"Who two?"

"Don't you 'who two' me, Owen! I wasn't born yesterday. Tell your good old Aunt Etta everything."

"Well, it's looking pretty good so far."

"Then what are you going to do about it?"

"About what?"

Etta balled up her tiny fist and gave me a pop right on the shoulder. "Owen Richards, you're pigheaded! What are you going to do about the Church? She's not going to touch you with a ten-foot pole until you do something about that."

That was the best thing about Etta—you couldn't get anything past her.

"Actually—"

"It's about time, honey."

"But I haven't said anything."

"You don't need to. You've said enough already. Have you set the date?"

"Kind of. Well, not exactly." I patted the pocket of my jacket, where my Message From Home card was, still without a date written on it. "You're the first person who knows. I want to get an idea of what Julianna's plans are before I set anything in concrete."

"I'm pleased for you, Owen. Very pleased." Etta took me by the arm and escorted me to the kitchen, where she had already set the table with three place settings of her best china. On each small plate was a chilled slice of apple pie. "Lewis will be thrilled."

"I'm sure he will be," I said.

"So will everyone else, honey."

"I know, but I want to do this on my own. I don't want Julianna to think I'm doing this for her."

"Are you?"

"No, I'm not," I said, formalizing the thought into words for the first time. "I'm doing this because it's right. I have deep feelings for Julianna, but I'm pretty certain about this independent of those feelings. I want to find the perfect time to tell her."

"Well, take my advice—there is no perfect time. Don't dillydally around." The always-pleasant Etta bit into a forkful of apple pie and scrutinized the taste. "Not as flaky as I'd like," she said, looking into space. It tasted perfect to me.

Julianna took forever to get back from her interview. I talked with Etta, and we shared ideas about religion and life. If she had been sixty-five years younger, Julianna would have had some competition. I told Etta that and she giggled like she was closer to nineteen than ninety.

When Julianna did get home, she was on fire.

"I got it!" she squealed as she jumped through the front door. "I got the job! I was the last interview and I got the job!" She pirouetted through the living room and into the kitchen, where Etta and I were still perched on kitchen chairs.

"Oh, honey," said Etta, getting up and giving Julianna a big hug. Not to be denied a chance to hug her, I got up and took my turn. She pried herself out of my arms and did another pirouette for good measure. After that hug, I was just about as giddy as she was.

"Congratulations, ma'am." I broke into a rousing rendition of the theme from *Green Acres.* "Farm living is the life for me . . ." Nobody cared for my yodeling.

"It's an inside joke," Julianna told a perplexed Etta. "Anyway, I start as soon as I can get things packed up and moved out here. I can't wait. Oh, Aunt Etta, this is the job I really wanted. I just didn't dare let myself get excited about it."

"I'm proud of you, sweetheart." Etta gave Julianna another big hug, and I got right back in line.

When the celebration started to die down, Etta looked at me, expecting me to share my big news. I subtly shook my head, not wanting to trump Julianna's announcement. From the sound of things, I was going to be seeing a lot more of her in the near future. There was time.

CHAPTER 7

I was expecting a night drive back around the point of the mountain so I could find the right moment to spring my good news on Julianna, but that was not to be. By the time we got done visiting with Etta and celebrating Julianna's success, it was well past midnight and Saturday morning had officially taken over. Etta talked us into staying at her place until after church on Sunday. How could I refuse?

There was a guest room for Julianna, and the couch in the living room pulled out into what torture experts from the Middle Ages might have loosely called a bed. I gave the bed a new nickname—"the rack," in deference to the bar that had become such an intimate part of my anatomy overnight. When morning came, I wished I'd slept in the bed of my Dodge.

"Good morning, Mary Sunshine," said Julianna, prancing into the living room.

"Morning," I said, sitting up on the bed. I ran my tongue around the inside of my mouth and decided I could use a toothbrush. "I need to run out and buy a couple of things. Is there a little store around here somewhere?"

"No need. Etta has supplied each of us with a brand-new toothbrush. Yours is sitting out on the bathroom counter."

"Maybe later I'll buy a new shirt."

"It's a date. How was the couch?"

"Great. I slept like never before." *More like never,* I thought, but wasn't about to admit that to Julianna. As far as she needed to know, everything was always going to be perfect.

"So, how did Sparky do?"

"That little weasel didn't move all night. The stench of his breath wafting up under the covers was the only sign of life. About a half hour ago he woke me up like a smelly cuckoo clock."

"No," said Julianna, digging for the little pest and scratching his chin, "like a lonely little poochski."

"Yeah, me and Sparky-doodle there. We're a couple of bad old bachelors." What I didn't want Julianna to know was that the only similarity between Sparky and me right then was our breath.

I shooed Sparky out from under the covers and off "the rack" so I could close the apparatus to await its next victim. Sparky wasn't happy about it, but I was glad to get the thing out of sight and out of mind.

After I got ready, putting Etta's gift of a toothbrush to work, I joined her and Julianna in the kitchen. All things of any importance happened in Etta's kitchen. In this case, the most important thing was good smells that promised my kind of breakfast. No grapefruit here.

"It's stuffed French toast," Etta said, holding a stack of them under my nose with a spatula.

"How do you stuff french toast?" I asked.

"You slap two pieces of cinnamon bread around a layer of cream cheese. It's Uncle Leon's secret recipe," said Etta, placing her hand over her heart.

"I never met Uncle Leon, but I think he's my new best friend." I loaded four of the delicious-looking things on my plate.

Julianna was already digging in. "We already blessed it," she said between mouthfuls.

"Yes, dear," said Etta. "We waited for you like one dog waits for another."

"That's okay. After the kind of culinary torture I've been exposed to at Al's, this is paradise."

I put my fork to good use during breakfast so Etta and Julianna could talk. Most of the conversation centered on Julianna's new job. I was just happy to be there, and distracted with the thought of how great it was going to be to tell Julianna my announcement. I was grateful to have one bit of good news in a sea of discouraging events at work.

I did the breakfast dishes, fighting Etta for position in front of the sink, while the two girls planned their attack on the weekend. Etta refused to come with us to bum around Provo, using homework as an excuse. She only winked at me three times as she pushed Julianna and me out the door.

Our first stop was to a clothing store in the mall. I had to try things on. No sacrifice was too great, though, and I survived—barely. I bought a new shirt and pair of pleated Dockers to replace the stale clothes I was wearing. Julianna was trying to talk me into staying in Provo one more night so I could go to church with her. I shelled out for a pair of slacks, a dress shirt, and a tie, finishing the outfit with a pair of leather dress shoes and a belt. I was set.

After that we spent some time on the BYU campus, stopping at the bookstore for a snack and then wandering around. Julianna dropped in on a few professors that she'd known from her undergraduate days and saw two other people she knew. By the time evening rolled around, we were both starving.

Back in Lindon we tried with all our persuasive powers to get Etta to come out to dinner with us. She just wouldn't budge, and she didn't volunteer the use of her kitchen either. Julianna and I both got the hint. Before we left, Etta gave me one of those shoulder shrugs that said, "Did you tell her?" There hadn't been a good time all day, so I just gave her a tiny shake of my head. She gave me a disgusted harrumph and told us to go to dinner someplace nice.

"You take this young lady to the Ruby River Steak House for a real, sit-down meal," she said. "Then maybe you two can talk." She couldn't have been more obvious if she'd held up a neon sign that said, "Get to work, plowboy."

Julianna freshened up and we set out for Ruby River. Everything was perfect; nothing was going to ruin this night.

* * *

"Didn't I see that car at the mall today?" I asked, more to myself than to Julianna. "That little brown Chrysler K-car." I pointed to a dark brown sedan with square fenders. It was parked in the lot at the Ruby River Steak House.

"Where? Oh, I don't know. Why?"

"Just . . . oh, never mind. I just haven't seen one of those around for a while." *At least not since I saw one just like it in the library parking lot at Park City,* I thought. I took a closer look at the car and memorized the license plate. It was a "Best Snow on Earth" plate starting with C-J-O. Kujo. I could remember that.

The atmosphere inside the restaurant was pleasant, the appetizers delicious, and the company divine. We started talking about how nice it was for Etta to put us up.

"She really likes you, Owen," Julianna said. "She told me that you and Lewis are her favorite nephews."

"That's quite a compliment considering I'm not her nephew."

"Don't try to tell her that."

The conversation stalled; it was now or never. If I could work my baptism into the conversation now, we could spend the rest of the evening celebrating. "Julianna, I have something I want to talk to you about."

"It sounds serious, Owen. What is it?"

"Hey, Julianna McCray," said a raspy voice from across the restaurant.

It was like someone had tied me to a stake and pushed a pike through my chest. A tall man with extra-curly black hair and a pocked face walked over to our table, leaned down, and gave Julianna a sideways hug.

"I haven't seen you in years. What are you doing here? The last I heard you were going back to Kansas City." He had a crusty voice, and he hadn't even acknowledged me yet.

"Hi, Rusty. It's so nice to see you," said Julianna. "Rusty, this is Owen Richards."

"Owen, glad to meet you." Rusty looked in my direction just long enough to shake my hand. Then his gaze went right back to Julianna as if I weren't even there.

"So, how long are you going to be in Provo?"

"Just another day or so."

Blah blah blah, I'm a software engineer. Blah blah blah, I make ten times what this clod sitting by you makes. Blah blah, I'd like to bury this guy in the back parking lot and marry you. Rusty was monopolizing my time with Julianna. She'd made a couple of half-hearted attempts to slip a word in, but Rusty was quite a conversationalist. All you had to do was ask him.

"Anyway, Julianna, I want to introduce you to my date." He looked around for a second. "There she is."

A very well-dressed and ritzy-looking woman with short black hair sauntered up to us from the ladies' room. She was holding a little black clutch purse in both hands, and she smiled gracefully when Rusty introduced all of us.

"This is Rhiana. We met in college, and she's in town for a few days on business. We thought we'd see the town." He said the word "town" in a rather derogatory tone, as if Provo, Utah, wasn't really much of a town at all. He also went out of his way to make sure he explained that Rhiana was only a casual date. The smarm alarm in my head went off so loud it was nearly deafening.

"Anyway, we just thought we'd come in for a quick bite. Have you guys eaten yet?" He looked at the half-finished plate of breaded mushrooms we'd been sharing and apparently a sixty-thousand-watt lightbulb went off in his head. "Say, I'd love to catch up with you . . . mind if we join you? Waiter, could you bring us two more places, please?"

No. No. Say it isn't going to happen. Julianna and I looked at each other as the waiter nodded and proceeded to bring two more place settings to our table. Mr. Smarmy and his date were actually going to sit with us.

Oh, please, please, Mr. Smarmy, have a heart attack or something. Don't let this happen.

But it did. Julianna, I could tell, was as put off as I was by Rusty. He kept her busy listening all through dinner, and I had a chance to get familiar with Briana, or Dee Anna, or Rhiana. Whoever she was, she was lot nicer than her date. She was a software technician for a company in Denver, and she was in town being trained on a new update in some fancy product that her company retailed. I found her to be gracious and interesting. How she got hooked up with the smarm man I would never have guessed. Until, that is, she very quietly told me that he represented the product her company sold, and then implied with a roll of her eyes that she accepted his dinner invitation out of courtesy. I liked Rhiana—but we had to ditch Smarmy.

By the time the main dish had been served and eaten, I could tell Julianna had had enough of Rusty. She'd tried to talk to Rhiana, but Rusty had things to say. When we got up to pay the bill and leave, I felt almost sorry for Rhiana. My eyes must have given that away because Rhiana smiled and told Rusty she had an early meeting and had to get back to her hotel. He said he wasn't aware of an early meeting, and she explained that she had a conference call meeting that she needed to prepare for. I smiled at her lie, and she gave me a wink as we walked out of Ruby River.

Rusty made one last-ditch effort to get a little more face-to-face time with Julianna. As we were putting on our coats, he said, "Well, we can't let the night go to waste. I know a place—"

Julianna cut him off. "Oh, I'm afraid I have to get home. We've had a long day, and I couldn't possibly stay out any longer."

Rusty opened his mouth so some more smarm could come out, but Julianna was ready for him. "It was great to see you again, Rusty. Now that I know you're in Provo, I'll be sure to look out for you."

Rusty almost had a chance to say good-bye before Julianna turned to me.

"Owen, I need to visit the rest room before we leave. Will you warm the truck up for us? Thanks." Julianna simply disappeared, leaving Rusty standing there speechless.

I said good-bye to Rhiana and silently wished her luck. Then I went out to the truck and watched the happy couple leave. When the coast was clear, I went back inside and stood in front of the ladies' room.

"He's gone," I said through the door.

Julianna slowly emerged from the rest room, looking around for Rusty.

"He really is gone," I assured her. "Ready to go home?"

"Home nothin'."

"But, I thought you were tired . . . had a hard day and all that. What's the matter? Were you trying to ditch poor Rusty?"

"He's just a little too hip-slickin' cool for me."

"Hip-slickin'? What's that?"

"Oh, get with it, Owen. Now, take me dancing."

"Your wish is my command, young lady. Dancing it is."

We left the restaurant and got into my truck, thanking Rusty that the truck's heater had ample time to cut the chill from the cab.

"You'll have to give me directions. There must be a bar or something around here that plays dancing music."

Julianna froze in place. "Did I just hear that? Did you just say that to me? I can't believe . . . were you talking to me? Were *you* talking to me? You must have been talking to me because I don't see anyone else in this truck."

"What?" I said innocently.

"Owen Richards, you will *not* be taking me to a bar. Not tonight and not any night."

Now it was my turn to freeze. I wasn't sure if she was joking or if I'd just blown the whole deal. "Did I say bar? I meant . . . bar . . . barber. I meant, I wonder if there's a barber around here so that when I take you dancing my hair will be neat and trimmed, just like a missionary's. That's what I said."

"Turn east on Center Street."

I did as I was instructed, hoping I wasn't in trouble after all.

I had noticed the brown K-car as we left the restaurant and then picked it up again as we got closer to Center Street. It seemed to be more than a little coincidental, but the car soon disappeared as we got into heavier traffic.

"Hey, wait a minute," I said as we neared the end of Center Street. "That's a state hospital over there. What kind of dancing did you have in mind?"

"We're going to Seven Peaks for some ice-skating. I think we can still use the ice. It's going to be used by the women's hockey teams during the Games."

"Skating? That's not dancing," I said. Oh, how wrong I was.

Julianna was a great skater—which meant that she could keep her feet under her in a pair of skates. More than that, she could skate backward and turn in little circles. I looked more like a newborn colt trying to get to its feet.

"Okay, now show me a triple lutz," I said, trying to impress Julianna with my skating talk.

"I would, but they had to rename that move the triple klutz after I perfected it."

"Man, these skates are killing my feet," I complained.

"Why don't you go get a bigger size?"

"Will they let me?"

"Of course. I'll baby-sit myself while you make the exchange."

I hobbled my way across the ice and to the skate rental area. The guy who exchanged my skates made a face like I was the millionth customer who didn't know his own shoe size.

"Thanks," I said, taking the bigger skates to a bench where I could sit down and lace them on. I wondered how many weird feet had visited the inside of these skates. Whatever their history, they fit much better, and I worked my way back to the ice on a set of more comfortable feet.

Julianna was on the other side of the rink with her back to me. She was standing still, but through the crowd I couldn't see what she was doing. I took a few tentative steps out onto the ice, staring at my feet just to stay upright.

I made some forward progress and ended up hugging the wall of the rink. I decided to wait for Julianna to pass me, and I raised my head to look at her again. She was talking to someone, no doubt another one of her many admirers. I admired her too. Julianna's head snapped back like she was laughing, and I caught a glimpse of the person she was talking to. He looked like . . . it couldn't be!

My heart rate doubled. I pushed away from the wall to get a better angle on the man. All at once I knew who it was. I dug my skates into the ice and ran as fast as I could toward Julianna. Unfortunately, this was against the flow of skaters. When I finally fell, momentum was on my side and I took several people with me onto the ice. I spun a few times before coming to rest, and it took me a second to reorient myself and find Julianna. She was alone, but she was looking at me. Then again, who *wasn't* looking at me?

I crawled upright and skated to her, out of breath, but the man she'd been talking to was gone. "Who was that?"

"I don't know. He said he thought he recognized me. He said he was a neighbor of Etta's."

"Where did he go?" I snapped.

"Owen, relax. He was just some neighbor. He left just before you performed that double axle out there. By the way, you're supposed to do that move in the air, not lying on the ice." She laughed.

"Julianna, where did he go?"

"Owen, what's wrong?"

I looked around, sure that I'd lost him. Raymond Hunt had been talking with Julianna right in front of me. Now he was gone. But I decided there was nothing to be gained by telling Julianna, figuring it would just scare her.

"Maybe I need to check myself into the state hospital next door."

"Maybe so. What did you have, a Rusty flashback?"

"Too much exposure to that smarmy character could drive anyone crazy."

"You could be right," Julianna said.

I decided I needed to make conversation before Julianna got suspicious. "So, where did you meet Rusty in the first place?" I looked around for Hunt.

"Oh," she said, "I went out with him when I went to the Y."

"You went out with him?"

"Once," she said. "It was a blind date, and it was awful. I think he still wants to marry me."

I was still looking into the crowds to see if I could find Hunt—if that's who it was. How could I be sure? I was starting to second-guess myself. Maybe it wasn't him.

With time, I got better at skating, and Julianna and I had time to talk and laugh. She was easy to be around, and I wished I'd been able to focus just on her, but I was too preoccupied with watching for Hunt to make the most of the evening.

My ankles thanked me when we took off the skates and headed back out to the truck. Julianna had a good time, but I could tell she was wearing out. She yawned, and I yawned back.

"Maybe we both need a good night's sleep."

"Yeah," I said, looking around the lot for the K-car. It never hurt to be just a little cautious.

"Are you okay, Owen?"

"Sure, I'm just tired."

"You look like you're nervous or something."

Thinking fast, I said, "Oh, at night I'm used to being really into what's going on around me. Occupational hazard." I was thinking fast, not well, but I hoped she bought it.

"I had a good night tonight, Owen," Julianna said as she climbed into the passenger seat. "It was fun."

I wasn't in the mood for small talk, but I did my best until we got back to Etta's. The right time to tell Julianna about my baptism hadn't materialized, and I could tell Etta was disappointed when Julianna didn't say anything about it. I was confident, though, that there would be another time.

Etta and Julianna talked about our date in the kitchen, and I snuck away to do a quick security survey of the house—just in case Etta's "neighbor" decided to come for a visit. The windows were new and all securely locked against the winter cold . . . and cold-blooded criminals. The outside doors all had sufficient and operational locks on them. From each window I could get a pretty decent view of the yard and neighboring houses. The neighborhood was new enough that the shrubs hadn't grown up over the windows. Even though the house seemed secure, I knew there were 101 ways someone could get into it if they wanted to. In fact, the more I thought about the "neighbor," the more I thought it really was Hunt. The best I could do was make sure no one got into the house that night.

It didn't take long for things to wind down, and eventually everyone retired to bed. I was pretending to sleep on "the rack," but as soon as I was sure that Etta and Julianna were both asleep, Sparky and I went on the prowl. I could watch the front door from the living room, but I couldn't see the laundry room door entry. I figured it was probably okay since I could hear that door fairly well. However, just to make sure . . .

I opened a few cupboards until I found what I was looking for, grateful that Etta was a chip eater. I poured half a bag of Fritos just inside the laundry room door to make sure that anyone who came in that way made a lot of noise navigating the chip field. The old-time movie private eyes used a broken light bulb, but I had to improvise.

The other half of the bag of chips came with me to my bed for nighttime rations. It was going to be a long one. I considered using them under each window, but figured the carpet would've dampened the sound effects and that would have been a waste of chips.

Etta, the new student, had a computer just off her kitchen, and on her computer table was just what I needed to further secure the house. I took half a dozen three-and-a-half-inch floppies and wedged them in the cracks above the interior doors. Each made a little shelf on which I placed a tin can (from the recycle bin) containing a handful of marbles from Grammy's toy basket. I didn't want anyone to be able to move through the house without me knowing; I was pretty proud of myself.

The doors were secure, but the windows still bothered me. Etta's windows were sliders and for the most part pretty secure. But I wasn't going to underestimate Hunt. I decided to use a variation of the door trick on the windows. I filled several large glasses with water and set them precariously on each windowsill. I placed each glass in such a way that if a window slid open, it would knock the glass off the sill and douse the person in bed underneath. The sounds produced after that would be a natural consequence and would suffice to alert me to a problem. I had to stand directly over Etta to do the window in her room. I thought she was going to wake up and scream, but it turned out she was a sound sleeper.

With the house thus secured, I sat in bed with Sparky and my chips—and we waited as I tried to talk myself out of thoughts that Hunt wasn't going to come, that he'd be crazy to come after I'd seen him. I pushed aside the fear that I'd booby-trapped the house for nothing.

I killed some time pacing the living room in the dark. When I got sleepy, I resorted to push-ups every half hour to keep the blood running. I kept up that routine all night, not daring to doze off.

The first sign of morning was the sun lighting the eastern sky behind the mountains. I decided it was time to defortify the house. That thought was followed by the realization that a string of natural consequences would make defortifying a moot point.

It was Etta who first felt the effects of my makeshift house of horrors. First she was doused with water from above when she reached up to let a little fresh air in. How was I supposed to know she liked fresh winter air in the morning? After Etta was done yelling, naturally, she charged out of her bedroom, where she was struck on the head by a tin can full of marbles. Now she was wet and injured. She chose to yell again.

By this time Julianna was awake and investigating, and she tripped her door can as well. She chose to scream. There was one bit of consolation, and that was that nobody was going to step in the Fritos and make a noise because Sparky was just licking up the last chip.

Lucy, you have some splainin' to do, I thought.

I told Etta I simply had a healthy preoccupation with the safety of my "girls" and got ready for church. Julianna knew a few of the details about my recent problems with Hunt, but she wasn't inclined to help me explain my security neurosis, what with her bruised head and all. It was a quiet morning, and I hadn't scored any points with anyone.

While Etta and Julianna took their sweet time getting ready for church, I had a quick breakfast of Raisin Bran and Pop-Tarts. I took a quick shower and dressed with plenty of time to regret not having put all my traps away earlier. Hunt hadn't come during the night, and for that I was thankful. Despite the embarrassment of having appeared like a total security flake, I decided that I was better safe than sorry.

While I was closing "the rack" and hoping that it was the last night of my life to be tortured on it, I saw a piece of plastic tubing on the floor underneath one of the bed rails. Reaching through the metal springs, I pulled it up and almost threw it into the toy basket before stopping to examine it. It was a "Mr. Microphone." The device consisted of a small microphone and radio transmitter in a plastic case. You could buy one at any toy store and transmit your voice over an FM radio signal. It ran on D batteries and was capable of transmitting twenty or thirty feet. It was a harmless child's plaything, but I realized the device was on. The first thing I thought of was Hunt. With a simple contraption like this, he could park outside and listen to everything that was said in the house on his car radio.

"Etta," I said, barging into the bathroom where she was getting ready.

"Owen!" she said, shocked that I'd dare to look at her without her face on.

"Have you seen this before?" I held the toy out in front of her.

"Owen, what's the matter?" Julianna came out of her room and stood in the bathroom doorway.

"Have you seen this toy before?" I repeated.

"No. Owen, can this wait?" asked Etta.

"You've never seen this before?"

"No." She looked more closely at the device. "No, I don't recognize it. The kids leave things here all the time, and . . ."

"Did you see it last time the kids were here?"

"Well," Etta was clearly shaken by my demeanor, "I don't remember it."

I left the bathroom and went directly out the front door, looking for the brown K-car. I circled the house, scanning down every block. Nothing.

When I got back into the house, Etta and Julianna were standing in the living room, both half ready.

"What was that all about?" asked Julianna.

"Nothing," I said. I didn't want to make yet another scene. "I thought I saw someone I knew."

Julianna gave me a long stare, and Etta just shook her head. They both retreated back into their rooms, and I sat on the couch, looking out the window for the K-car. I sat that way until we left for church.

Church was held in a neat and orderly building (albeit sparse by my Protestant standards). Just entering the edifice reaffirmed my decision to be baptized. I simply felt good about it. Today I would tell Julianna that I had decided to be baptized, and after that announcement, scaring Etta to within an inch of her life would be forgotten.

Because I'd managed to stay awake for the better part of the night, I wasn't at my best at church. I was still wary of Hunt and the brown K-car, but I thought church would be a relatively safe place. I fell asleep during the first speaker (his fault, not mine) and barely made it through the concluding speaker. Julianna noticed.

Sunday School held my interest because we attended a new members' class taught by the missionaries. However, I didn't say much or volunteer to answer questions because I was just too tired. I spent priesthood meeting in a daze watching the elders talk about raising kids. It was all over my head. By the end of the last hour, I was spent.

Things were still a little tense on the way home. I was more worried about what Hunt may have been doing while we were away than I was about Julianna's attitude. I did a sweep of the house when we arrived and made sure there were no obvious signs of a burglary. Julianna changed clothes, and we got ready to drive back up to Salt Lake. I worried about Etta's safety, but decided to trust that Hunt would follow me rather than mess with her. It was a semi-risky assumption, but it was either that or call the cops. In the end, even if I did call the cops, they wouldn't be able to protect Etta short of moving her into a safe house, and they weren't going to do that because a crazy cop from Salt Lake who wasn't even stable enough to work thought he saw a ghost.

"Would it be alright if we drove up the canyon and went to Salt Lake the back way, through Heber City and Park City?" I asked when we left in the truck.

"If you don't mind," said Julianna, "can we just go up the freeway? I'd like to get back early." She seemed a bit subdued.

"Sure," I said, cringing inwardly. I had wanted a romantic drive through scenic country to set the mood for my baptism disclosure. Now I'd have to find a romantic stretch of Interstate 15. There wasn't one. By the time I'd worked up my courage, we were sitting in the truck in front of her friend's house on Fort Union Boulevard.

"Julianna, I'd like to talk to you about something."

"I know, Owen. Me, too."

"By all means, ladies first." I wanted the last spot on the schedule so that we could revel in the wonderfulness of my announcement.

"Owen, I've had a great time with you. I'm glad we had a chance to stay in Lindon. But . . ."

This conversation wasn't having a stellar start.

I could see she was working up her courage, and she finally said, "I think we need to talk about where all this is going."

Better. I could manage this.

"I think you're right," I said, hoping to turn this conversation around.

"I really like you, and you're a good friend."

I nodded, knowing exactly where this was going.

"When Lewis died," she continued, "I don't know what I would have done without you."

"I feel the same way. You have no idea."

"But this isn't what I want. All my life I've dreamed of a certain . . ." She didn't finish.

"Stop for a second," I said. "I have something to tell you."

Julianna shook her head. "No, don't tell me. I don't want to hear it. I can't. I can't see you anymore." She dropped it on me like a three-megaton bomb. "I thought at first that something would work out, but I can't go on this way. I do care for you, Owen. I really do. But ever since I was a little girl I've dreamed that . . . that . . ."

She was crying now—sobbing. I couldn't even speak. When she'd collected her herself, she went on. "It's important for me to marry in the temple and to raise a family with a . . ."

"A member of the Church," I finished for her.

"Yes."

"Julianna, let me tell you something. I'm—"

"No, Owen. There's nothing you can tell me that will change the way I feel. I'm falling in love with you, but I can't let that happen. This issue is non-negotiable. Owen, I'll call you and we can talk some more. I still value our friendship."

Julianna opened the door and got out. I was so stunned that I just sat there. She didn't turn around until she reached the front door. Then she gave me a short wave and turned away.

* * *

I stopped by my apartment and picked up some fresh clothes before driving up the canyon to Al's place. It was just late enough in the twilight that the light was fading and about half the cars had their headlights on. I drove in a daze, wondering how I could resurrect my relationship with Julianna.

I could have told her about my baptism plans, but that would have sounded desperate after her news. I had wanted so badly to insulate my decision to be baptized from a situation like this, knowing that if I had revealed my plans, all her life she'd wonder if I did it for me or for her. That wasn't fair to either of us. I loved Julianna—nothing could be clearer to me. But I couldn't muddy the waters by promising to be baptized under what could be considered emotional duress. What was I supposed to do now? I didn't realize how far I'd driven past Al's place before I decided to turn around and head back.

Chalise Porter at KSOP radio said that it was approaching nine o'clock and that the news would follow the next three songs. I listened past a few inane commercials until the music started again. The first song was by a guy with a deep, cavernous voice who wanted to talk about himself. I barely made it through that one. The second was by three women who sang about a girl with twenty-three personalities. You're telling me. It was the third song that sent me over the edge. It was the one Julianna had been singing at the car wash. I turned the radio off.

"Oh, Chalise. You're killing me here."

After a lonely drive back down the old highway, I parked my truck between two cars in Dan's grocery store lot. The cars on either side both cost more than a year's salary for me, and I marveled at the opulence that still existed in this tiny mountain valley long after the silver money had disappeared. The grocery store was a good place to be around people and be anonymous at the same time, a feeling I was strangely comfortable with right then. Inside, last-minute Sunday shoppers pushed their carts up and down the aisles. I'd given up shopping on Sundays, but on this day, I didn't care. I wasn't hungry either, but I threw a couple of four packs of Hostess Cupcakes in my basket. I started to walk away, then went back for another four pack. After I was sure I had enough artificial food to get me through my ordeal, I made my way to the check-out line.

I left the store and mindlessly negotiated the road to Al's place, then turned into his driveway. I rumbled onto the concrete slab and waved to Calvin, who was standing on his front porch. "No shoveling?" I yelled to him as I got out of the cab.

"Sunday," was his reply. "Al does it himself on Sundays."

I felt a pang of regret as I picked up my grocery bag off the seat and walked inside. I hoped Calvin wasn't watching me. I turned to see, and as I did I noticed the house across the street. I stopped and scrutinized the front of it. Something was different. What was it?

Calvin saw me and turned to look at the house, too. I shook my head and went inside, leaving Calvin to wonder what I was doing. Something wasn't quite right.

Al was in his den and not paying any particular attention to me, so I casually walked with my little grocery bag down to my room and closed the door, deciding it was better if Al didn't actually *see* me eat a Hostess Cupcake because he might've fallen victim to a health food conniption. In the privacy of my room, I very quietly pulled open my brown paper bag and retrieved a package of cupcakes. I rolled the bag closed again and shoved it behind a pillow.

The cupcakes were factory wrapped in cellophane. It's hard to be sneaky with cellophane. Slowly pulling apart the seamed edge, I rescued my confection from its airtight prison. Instead of crumpling the packaging, I neatly flattened it and placed it gently between the pages of one of Al's *Outdoor Life* magazines on the nightstand. If he came in the room, I didn't want evidence lying about.

Hostess Cupcakes, which consist of all man-made ingredients, are the eighth wonder of the modern world. Nothing is so moist, nothing so satisfying. And they defy age. If the world were to come to an end in a catastrophic event, Hostess Cupcakes would survive. Al and his Mormon friends might have mountains of red wheat and honey in white plastic buckets, but I would have a truckload of nearly indestructible Hostess Cupcakes.

I was sitting on the floor absorbed in my naughty little diet and contemplating my not-quite-perfect life, so I didn't notice Al open the guest room door. His eyes went wide when he saw my cheeks bloated with devil's food pseudo-cake and the telltale white, creamlike filling in the corners of my mouth. I thought he might scream like a teenage girl at a horror movie.

Slowly, a gleam began to develop in his eyes and the corners of his lips rolled up. I just sat there, watching him. By the time he started to laugh, I felt as guilty as a third grader with the answers to the weekly spelling quiz written on my palm. I tried to speak, to offer an explanation, but all that came out was cake crumbs. Al started to laugh so loud I thought he might attract unwanted attention from the neighborhood busybody.

"Okay, okay," I managed to mumble through the black tar in my mouth. "I'm beak, I ab-mib ib."

"You're what?" Al asked through near tears.

"I'm beak." I forced a tremendous lump of cake down my esophagus and tried again. "I said, I'm weak, I admit it." I ran my tongue around my mouth to help clear the black-tar cupcake residue and swallowed again.

Al was able to bring himself under control, but he couldn't force the big, fat smile from his face. "You're right, pal. That's the most pathetic thing I've seen in hours—and I work nights, so you know what I see *then.*"

The shame was unbearable, so I reached behind the pillow, picked up my bag full of Hostess Cupcake four packs, and squished it into a huge cake ball. Then I threw it as hard as I could at Al. He caught the bag on his chest and uncrumpled it, looking inside at the mess. Then it was as if the four winds flew out of Pandora's box and hit him in the face. He dropped the bag on the floor and started to guffaw again, laughing so hard he fell into the hallway. I kicked the door closed and sat down hard on the bed. Al must have been rolling on the floor near my room because I could still hear him even after I sandwiched my head between two pillows. How humiliating. I had just been caught smuggling contraband artificial food into the house of my very nutritionally conscious friend and attempting to eat it in unprecedented quantities. The evidence was still smeared on my cheeks. As a snapshot of life, it was nothing to brag about. And, yes, I ate a few smashed-up cupcakes after Al left.

Not long after that, Al knocked softly on my door and opened it.

"I'm leaving for work in a few. You okay?"

I nodded, not sure what to say.

"Are you sure?" he asked, walking into the room and sitting on the end of the bed.

I shrugged. "Julianna gave me the ol' heave-ho tonight."

"Ouch. Someone else?"

"No, she was just doing what she thought was right. Man, I hate that."

"Hate what?"

"That she was doing what she thought was right and now I can't even be mad at her." I sat up. "She doesn't want to get too close to someone outside the Church."

Al started to say something and then hesitated, trying to find the right words. "Do you know why she feels that way?" he asked.

"Yes, and I don't blame her. In fact . . ." I couldn't keep it a secret any longer. "I understand too well. I've been seeing the missionaries, and I've committed to be baptized."

Al responded very slowly, a huge smile growing on his face. "You dog!" he said. "How long has this been going on?"

"A couple of months now. I just didn't want to get everyone all stirred up about it. I wanted it to be my decision."

"You sly dog. And you didn't tell her?" he asked, astonished. "Why didn't you say something?"

"I couldn't. Listen to how it would sound, 'Oh, you're dumping me because I'm not Mormon? Oh, then I'll just convert so we can live happily ever after.'"

"I see. So what you're saying is that you putzed around too long and now she's decided to cut bait." Al was pretty unsympathetic considering my misery.

"Yeah, something like that." I fell back on the bed. "I blew it."

"I suppose I can understand your not wanting to tell Julianna right away, but you could have said something to me."

"Yeah, I probably should have. I just wanted this to be my own decision. The irony here is that we're all doing the right things for the right reasons, and now everyone is hurt."

"Hang in there, Owen. You can still tell her about your baptism. She'll come around."

"Yeah, maybe."

"Have a little faith, bud. When is it?"

"When is what?"

"The baptism. When is the baptism?"

"I haven't . . . I mean, I don't know the exact date yet. I have a few details to work out."

Al sounded serious. "It wouldn't hurt to schedule it and see what happens."

I thought about the little card in my coat pocket. "Yeah, you're right. I'll let you know. Right now I'm too busy wallowing in self-pity and loneliness."

Al laughed softly and shook his head. "Lonely? You're not alone, Owen. Never."

"I know. It just feels that way sometimes."

"Let me give you some advice," Al said.

"What? More ancient aikido wisdom?"

"Much better. There are more people on your side in this situation than you realize."

"And what exactly does that mean?" I asked.

"It means don't be surprised if someday an army of angels riding chariots of fire steps up to fight your battles for you." Al got up and walked to the door. There were cupcake crumbs on the floor in front of it. He picked one up between his thumb and forefinger. "If ye have the faith of a cupcake crumb, ye can do all things." We both laughed. "Just have a little faith," he said as he walked out.

I sat on the bed for a while longer, regretting not having told Al earlier, as well as Julianna for that matter. I also wondered why I hadn't been able to set a baptism date. Maybe I was just afraid.

I heard Al open the garage door to leave.

"Owen!" he yelled. "Would you shut all the blinds? It looks like it's going to be a cold one. Oh, and remember to check your e-mail; it's been a few days, and LeJeune called while you were gone."

"Sure," I yelled back, and I heard the garage door shut. I went upstairs to the den, where I could see the driveway from the window. I watched Al's headlights swing out of the driveway and disappear down the street.

I typed the appropriate commands on Al's keyboard and accessed my e-mail account. There were a ton of messages, mostly junk mail. At least someone was thinking of me. I waded through dozens of inane ads, deleting most of them, until I got to one with no subject listed.

I clicked on it and watched a new screen open. A graphic was downloading line by line, and I didn't have to see very much before I could tell what the picture was. Sitting on the kitchen table in my condo, placed neatly on a copy of Sunday morning's *Deseret News,* was my cap—my original Mariners upside down-trident baseball cap.

CHAPTER 8

I left the den, not bothering to log off my e-mail account, and put on my jacket. Hunt had gone too far. This was no sick joke perpetrated by a coworker. Hunt was out there—I could feel him. He was never far away. I was determined to find him, and then . . . I'd cross that bridge when I got to it.

I needed to call LeJeune. I needed to call Al. I at least needed to report this to someone. But I quickly thought again. I was already on thin ice with the police department, and all they needed was one more excuse before they'd have me working the copy machine in the records division until my retirement party.

I stalked into the family room, my hands clenched into tight balls and my teeth grating against each other. I passed the large picture window that looked out over the lights of Park City. A fleeting thought interrupted my rage—Al had asked me to close the blinds. The blinds. That was it. The blinds.

I ran to the front door and swung it open. I could see the front of the house across the street, and there in plain sight was that little something that just wasn't right. The blinds in an upper window were open just slightly. They hadn't been that way before, I was sure.

Anger coursed through my veins like a flood of fire, and I had to work to subdue it. I'd learned through experience that anger was one of the most counterproductive emotions a police officer could submit to. I had to gain some control over my emotions so I could think.

I went back inside and closed the door. From the window, I could see the slightly opened blinds across the street. I looked at them again, trying to decide what to do.

After giving the situation some thought and giving myself time to cool off, I went out to my truck to retrieve my fanny pack. The fanny pack contained everything I'd need for a day on the job: a flashlight, handcuffs, a cell phone, a trauma bandage, my badge, and, hidden in a rear flap, my pistol.

It was a dark, starless night, but the streetlights reflected off the new snow and illuminated the neighborhood. I didn't see any tracks leading to or from the front of the empty house, and that made the open blinds even more suspicious. I put a hand over my fanny pack to reassure myself.

The house was on a curved portion of the street, so I was able to see two sides without intruding on the property. I couldn't make out footprints on either of the sides facing the street, but that didn't rule out the possibility that someone was coming and going from the back side.

I walked across the street as if I were going to use the far sidewalk and turned the corner around the house, really just wanting to get a closer view. As I rounded the bend, I identified the best approaches to the house, but continued walking up the street as if I were out for an evening stroll. There was a thicket of trees and dense shrubs between the target house and the one farther up the street, so I decided that on my return trip past the house, I would slip into the backyard using the shrubs as concealment. They would also conceal the footprints I would inevitably leave in the snow. Near the lee side of the closest thicket, the new snow hadn't covered the old crusted snow, so I planned a walking route close enough to the evergreens to avoid leaving obvious tracks.

I walked another three blocks up the street, thinking about what I'd seen on my first pass. When I'd gone far enough to satisfy any nosy neighbors of my innocent stroll, I returned the way I came. I stopped briefly near the bushes I wanted to duck into and pretended to look out over the valley between the houses.

I didn't see any curious faces peering through windows and felt relatively safe when I ducked into the shrubs. The crusted snow made more noise than I had anticipated, and as a result, I found myself hurrying to get to the backyard. I left a few footprints in the snow, but nothing could be done about that. A person looking specifically for evidence of trespassers would have easily seen my prints, but the casual observer wouldn't notice much.

The back of the house was fairly private, enclosed by the close hillside and thick stands of trees. I saw immediately what I suspected I'd find. Someone had been coming and going using a back entrance. I had to use my flashlight to be sure, but I could barely make out faint footprints leading to a window on the back side of the house. Fresh prints also led to and from the back door. And I knew they weren't made by the boy next door. Hunt had been there, and recently.

* * *

I examined the windowsill and found tool marks that had probably been made several days earlier. The freshest set of tracks led toward the window, and there was no evidence of anyone leaving. The window appeared to be the initial entry point and after that, the back door had been used for access to the house. Given the posh neighborhood I was in, I was surprised that an alarm hadn't been tripped on the initial entry. Either Hunt had defeated the alarm or it wasn't turned on. Since neither Al nor Calvin had noticed any activity in the house over the last few days, it was clear that whoever was visiting didn't want the neighborhood to know it.

I retreated into the trees, pushing myself into a dense stand of brush to get a better look at the rear of the house and to think.

There was only one explanation for all this, and it was Raymond Hunt. He was watching me. By now he probably knew most of my daily habits and routines. He may or may not have known about my situation at work, but I had to assume he knew I hadn't been to work tonight. I wondered just what else he knew about me. The thought made me queasy.

Obviously Hunt had been stalking me for some time now and had probably been watching me at my condo in Salt Lake too. I couldn't guess his ultimate plan, but I knew that whatever it was, it spelled bad news for me. So far, he'd had every advantage. But I determined that his mistake with the blinds was going to be the beginning of his undoing. I could feel it. Or was this yet another trap for poor, oblivious me?

* * *

I stayed in the trees for almost an hour hoping Hunt would show himself either coming or going. Eventually the cold earth beneath me did a good job of sucking the warmth from my body. If I'd been prepared, I'd have found a way to stay off the ground, but I was sitting in the snow and beginning to get stiff.

Going inside the house alone was foolish. It was unprofessional, and worse, it was against the law. I thought about those things briefly as I pried the already-breached window open and crawled inside. Dropping to the basement floor, I made enough noise to alert anyone in the house to my presence. I looked for a spot behind an old sofa near the window and hid. About fifteen minutes later, after no one came to investigate the noise at the window and my eyes adjusted to the darkness, I decided to move.

I moved slowly, one quiet footfall at a time, toward a hallway through what appeared to be a basement family room. I took baby steps so I could control the weight I placed on each foot, knowing that one secret to walking quietly was to test each step before fully committing to an exchange of body weight from one foot to the other. I wanted to see if I were stepping on something noisy before it was too late. If I did find that I was going to make noise, I could gently rock back on the original foot and choose another place to step. What a beautiful theory.

Theories are nice, but they often don't take reality into consideration. I walked slowly down the hall and into the rooms downstairs, checking each one for signs of an intruder, but my wet shoes made so much noise that I eventually decided that speed was a better tactic than stealth. Besides, walking slowly was taxing my leg muscles, and I couldn't keep it up indefinitely. Patience is also far more difficult in reality than in theory.

With that in mind, I charged up the stairs at a fast walk—just fast enough to surprise a bad guy, but not so fast that I couldn't respond to a threat. I held my pistol out in front of me, aiming at everything I looked at. In a matter of moments I cleared the rest of the house and didn't find Hunt. What I did find, however, was worse.

The room at the front of the house where the blinds were open was a large, empty bedroom. A spotting scope mounted on a small tripod sat back from the window in the shadows so it couldn't be seen from the outside. It was aimed at the front of Al's house.

I conducted a secondary search, this time looking more closely at places a person could be. I checked under every sink and opened every pantry door to see if Hunt was hiding somewhere. The floor plan had connecting rooms that allowed circular movement around the house. Unfortunately, this meant I couldn't clear areas ahead of me without diligent concern for what was behind me. It made my job more difficult, but I took my time and searched every possible hiding place. I even checked an attic crawl space accessed through a ceiling hatch above the main hallway. There was no sign of Hunt.

After I was sure he wasn't in the house, I performed yet another search, this time looking for evidence. The rooms were empty, and I didn't find anything that would lead me to him.

I'd been through the house several times now, and so it didn't take me long to check every door and window to make sure they were secure. The last place I went in the house was to the upstairs room where the telescope was set up, aimed at Al's house. I wanted that scope. It was the only piece of evidence I had, and I needed something to prove I wasn't cracking up. Hunt's fingerprint on it might save my career.

It was still relatively dark in the house, although my eyes had adjusted and I could see pretty well. I walked up the stairs to the upper level and went into what I remembered being the room with the telescope. When I didn't see the scope, I thought for a moment I'd been mistaken. I went back into the hall and looked for a doorway into another similar room. There wasn't one. My face flushed, and adrenaline coursed through me like a wave of nausea. I darted back into the bedroom and saw three indentations in the plush carpet where the tripod had been. The scope was gone.

I left the house by the back door at a run and easily picked up Hunt's fresh tracks in the new snow. From the distance between footfalls, I could tell he'd been running too. He couldn't be far ahead of me. I followed the tracks through the neighbors' yards and out to the street.

I stopped at the sidewalk four houses up from the target house, where the footprints ended and a set of tire tracks began. The narrow tire tracks belonged to a small car—a brown Chrysler K-car, undoubtedly.

From where Hunt had parked, I knew he could see enough of the front of Al's house to know which cars were in the driveway and what lights were on. Hunt was no fool. It was a great surveillance spot—but now I had *him* on the run.

* * *

I went straight to my truck and pulled out of Al's driveway without even a hint of a rational plan. I had no idea where I was going or what I intended to do, but I knew I had to think logically—and fast. Hunt had probably been watching me for a long time, since before I moved up to Al's. The only place I could think to find him was somewhere near my condo.

It was well into the wee hours of the morning and traffic was light, so I made good time down the canyon and pulled into my parking lot within twenty minutes. I couldn't think of a good way to sneak into my apartment so I decided to approach the front door casually, as if I were just arriving home late. I passed Mrs. Warneke's front window and noted a dim light coming from her living room. She'd probably fallen asleep in her chair after *The Late Late Show.*

The front door appeared secure, locked tight just like I'd left it. I opened it slowly and felt a cold draft from inside. I made a mental note to do as Al suggested and just move out altogether. As soon as I settled things with Hunt—one way or another—I'd do that.

I walked into my condo carefully, wary of any sound or movement. I was also concerned about booby traps. With that in mind I left the lights off, knowing that electricity was the prankster's playground. Using my flashlight judiciously, I examined each room of the house, but as far as I could tell, everything was the way I left it.

The only place in the house the dust had been disturbed was in a small hutch just off the kitchen where my computer had once been. The machine itself was on a permanent vacation with the FBI, likely getting the forensic examination of its life. I examined the phone jacks in each room to see if anything was plugged in where it shouldn't be, but aside from the kitchen phone, they were all empty—just like they were when the FBI checked for the same thing.

I wandered into the living room, scrutinizing the couch for more booby traps and, finding none, threw myself down to revisit some of the anger I'd felt about Hunt on the drive down the hill.

"I know a frame-up when I see one," I told the semidarkness, but got no answer. "You had me pegged as a patsy from the beginning, didn't you?" I nearly screamed. I took a pillow from the couch, swung it around, and let go. It flew into a floor lamp, knocking it into the wall with a loud crash.

A moment later, I heard a soft knock at the door. My pulse raced. It was just before 5:00 A.M., and I couldn't imagine who would be visiting at that hour. I looked through the peephole expecting to see Al, the only sane person who would be up and about at this time of the morning, but I was surprised to see little Mrs. Warneke shivering in her bathrobe on my doorstep.

Opening the door, I said, "Come in, Mrs. Warneke. I'm sorry I woke you. I was just a little upset." Our condos shared a wall, and occasionally I'd hear Mrs. Warneke's TV on late or she'd call me if my music was too loud. She was one of those great nosy neighbors.

"Oh, you didn't wake me. I'm sorry to visit so early, but I heard you up."

"I'm glad you're here; come on in." Forgetting about electrical booby traps, I flipped on the light switch, and instead of a huge explosion, the light came on.

Mrs. Warneke stepped gingerly into my entryway, pulling her bathrobe tightly around her. "I've been worried about you Owen. I haven't seen you in days. Is everything okay?"

"Yes, of course, Mrs. Warneke. I've been staying with a friend in Park City. I should have told you." I closed the door but didn't latch it, knowing that Mrs. Warneke wouldn't be comfortable shut in a man's apartment in her bathrobe.

"Oh? You have friends up the canyon? I shouldn't have worried; you're a big boy. For heaven's sake, you're a policeman."

If only that made a difference, I thought. "You have every right to worry, Mrs. Warneke. You're my mom away from home, you know."

Mrs. Warneke giggled like a schoolgirl. "Well, if everything is okay, I'll go back home. I just wanted to check on you." She gave me that look that said she really didn't think everything was okay, but she was too polite to pry.

"Thanks, Mrs. Warneke. Everyone needs a neighbor like you."

"Well, that's so nice of you to say, Owen." Mrs. Warneke pulled the door open and stepped out into the cold, taking a few steps toward her apartment. "I just got a little worried when your cousin came to see you and you weren't here, that's all."

"My cousin? Do you mean Lewis's cousin? Julianna? She's tall and has long red hair."

Mrs. Warneke was almost to her front door, but she stopped and turned around. "*He* definitely was not a *she,* and he didn't have red hair. He said he was *your* cousin dear, not Lewis's. I saw him going in your front door so, naturally, I asked him who he was."

The cold outside was nothing compared to the icy blast that Mrs. Warneke's words sent coursing through my veins.

"When?" I asked, trying to keep my composure.

"Oh, several days ago, probably not more than a week." Mrs. Warneke was shaking her head. "Why? Is something wrong, Owen? He was a nice man, and very handsome," she said. "Not much of a family resemblance, but he was polite."

"What did he look like?"

"Taller than you. Maybe a bit younger. He had brown hair. Sturdy build, like a farmer or worker. He had a friendly smile." Mrs. Warneke took a few steps toward me. "What's wrong?"

"I don't have a cousin like that."

"Oh my," said Mrs. Warneke, obviously upset.

I definitely didn't want to upset her. "I'm sorry. I was just thinking . . . It's okay, Mrs. Warneke. Now I remember. I think it was a different cousin . . . or something."

"Owen, I may be the weird old lady next door, but I'm no fool. If something's wrong—and I know there is—you simply need to . . ."

I knew what she was going to say. Mrs. Warneke was a woman with a strong and simple faith. She was going to tell me to pray or read the Bible.

". . . ask yourself, what would Jimmy Rockford do?" said Mrs. Warneke.

"Jimmy Rockford?"

"Yes, what would Jimmy Rockford do? I've seen every rerun of the *Rockford Files.* What would Jimmy Rockford do?"

Mrs. Warneke, my heavenly neighbor, shuffled into her apartment and shut the door.

Hmm, I thought, *Jimmy Rockford?*

With that thought in mind, I went back into my apartment and went through each room again, but found nothing.

What would Jimmy Rockford do? Shaking my head, I said to the wall between Mrs. Warneke's apartment and mine, "Jimmy Rockford would flip a cigarette in Hunt's face and punch him in the stomach. But I don't smoke, and Hunt isn't here to get punched."

I turned out the lights again and opened all the blinds in the apartment. Standing back from the glass, I looked for places where Hunt may have established a surveillance post of my condo. The predawn light was just beginning to brighten the sky behind the mountains, exaggerating the shadows between buildings, and I knew he was out there somewhere. *He could be watching right now. In fact,* I thought, *he could have the whole place wired.*

I decided to scour the condo for a hidden microphone. It looked so easy on TV—you just peek in the nearest lampshade and, voilà, you'd find a small electronic bug. I ended up taking off all the cover plates over my wall switches and outlets, figuring those were likely places for hidden microphones. So far, Hunt had been even more obvious than that. My gut told me that the Mr. Microphone at Etta's was his work.

Over an hour later, I was standing in the living room with a screwdriver, a handful of minuscule screws, and no little electronic bugs. The last cover I took off was to the phone jack my computer had been hooked up to. Expecting to hit pay dirt, I was disheartened to find that everything behind the plug looked normal. Just a bunch of wires.

It was just past seven-thirty, so Al would be either just leaving work or hanging around talking to the day-shift sergeant. I called the police department and, after navigating the most frustrating automated phone tree on the planet, finally got a human voice who told me that Al wasn't in the building.

I tried his house, but hung up when I got the machine. When I called his cell, I got a message that he was either outside his calling area or was unavailable. On the off chance that Al was already home and asleep, I decided to call Calvin's house and see if he could tell if Al was home. I opened my phone book and realized I'd never bothered to learn Calvin's last name. It took three tries to get a cooperative telephone operator to search through addresses in Park City to find the number for the house adjacent to Al's. It took all the charm I could muster.

"Hello?" Calvin answered.

"Hey neighbor, is Al home?"

"You must have the wrong number."

"No, wait Calvin. I mean is Al, your neighbor, at home yet? Have you seen any sign of him?"

"Who is this?"

"It's me, Owen. Owen Richards."

"Oh. Good morning, Mr. Richards. I don't know if Al is home."

"Is his car there?"

There was a pause. "I don't know. It didn't snow much last night, so I haven't been over there, and I can't see into the garage."

"Do me a favor, Calvin. Would you go over to Al's place and see if he's home? It's important."

There was a pause, then a reluctant, "Sure."

I gave Calvin my phone number and told him to call me back regardless. Then I waited.

I wasn't really sure what I was in such a hurry for, and I thought several times that all I was doing was dragging Al into another of my foolish, paranoid fantasies. But this time I had a witness. Mrs. Warneke had actually seen Hunt. I was sure she'd recognize Hunt's photo if I needed her to save my reputation.

When the phone rang again, I snatched it up before it could finish one full ring.

"Hello?"

"Hi." It was Calvin.

"Is he there?"

"No."

"Did you check?"

"No, I did some yoga on the front porch and just kind of felt a vacant aura about the house."

"Funny. So, he's not there?"

"Nope."

"Okay, listen. Will you do me a favor? When he gets home, tell him that I need him down here right away."

"Where's here?"

"At my condo in Salt Lake."

"I've got school."

"Oh, yeah. Okay, never mind. Hey, thanks man," I said.

"No problem."

"Bye." I dropped the phone from my ear and started to hang up.

"Hey, Owen!" Calvin yelled in the receiver.

I was just able to hear him as I moved to hang up. "What?"

"You should get that fixed."

"What fixed?"

"Your modem is picking up before you do. It's kind of hard on the ears."

"Modem? What ears?" I asked.

"My ears. I heard it just before you picked up. I can even hear some clicking now."

"Modem?" I asked again.

"Your computer is answering before you do," Calvin explained. "You must have it set up wrong. I could fix it. Cheap."

"Calvin," I said slowly, looking at the empty space where my computer used to be. "I want you to explain something for me—very slowly, and with little, tiny, non-computer guy words."

* * *

Calvin was going to make a great teacher someday. By the time he'd finished telling me what he'd heard and what it meant, I knew a thimbleful more about computers and telephones than I'd known before. It was enough.

I raced out the front door and ran down the steps to the mechanical room on the ground floor. The room housed the main electrical breakers for the building and the telephone punch boards. The door was locked.

I backed up and focused on a spot just beside the doorknob. Aiming my foot at the spot, I charged the door. It flew back on its hinges on the second kick and, thankfully, I lost all feeling in my foot, so there was very little pain. Inside the small mechanical room on a large rectangular panel was a web of small wires and switches.

It didn't take long for me to find the modem—a small, flat piece of computer hardware about the size of a ham sandwich temporarily wired to the phone punchboard along with the wires to my phone line. I picked it up and started to yank it out of the panel and then stopped myself. This was my only link to Hunt. I wasn't going to make it that easy for him to hide. I had a better idea.

I ran back to my apartment and dialed Calvin's number on the phone. The phone rang several times before someone answered.

"Hello?" said a polite feminine voice.

"Hello, Mrs. . . . Mrs. Calvin's mom. Can I talk to Calvin?"

"Who is this?" She suddenly wasn't so friendly sounding.

"This . . . is . . . this is Owen. I need to ask Calvin a question about my homework."

"Oh, okay." I could hear Mrs. Calvin yell for her son to pick up from somewhere else in the house. She told him it was someone who was late with his homework.

"Hello?" Calvin sounded a little confused.

"Calvin . . ."

"Homework, huh? I didn't know you guys had homework."

"Calvin, listen. About that modem—can you find out where it's sending its messages?" I could almost sense Calvin's computer hacker grin spreading across his young face.

"Well, that depends. Are you asking me to just do what I can, or are you asking me to walk around a few state and federal laws?"

"Calvin, as a police officer, I'm ordering you to find out where that modem is making its connections. Walk around whatever laws you have to."

"I heard you weren't still a cop."

"I'm still a cop. Quit messing with me, Calvin, or I'll tell your mom you've been hacking at my house when you were supposed to be shoveling."

"Dude, you're brutal. Well, maybe there's a callback set up on the modem. I'll take a look. Stay off your phone for a while; I'll call you back at exactly eight."

I disconnected with Calvin and stood facing the phone in my apartment. It rang a few times and then was quiet. I had so much nervous energy running through me I wanted to do jumping jacks, so I forced myself to sit on the chair and think happy thoughts.

The minutes ticked by, and at eight o'clock the phone rang right on schedule.

"Calvin?"

"Yeah."

"What do you have?"

"The modem receives calls from a number that comes back to the house across the street from here and an address really close to yours in Salt Lake. Whoever is on the other end of this thing is into everyone's phone."

"Figures," I said.

"And the modem calls Al's place once in a while. I checked the phone company records."

"That's breaking the law, isn't it?" I said, knowing the answer.

"It's okay, I dialed through the modem. No one but you will ever know it was me. Piece of cake."

"Calvin, you're a peach. I owe you a big one."

"Sure. Whatever you're doing, I hope it's important."

"You better believe it. I'll tell you all about it later. Now, if you see Al, let him know what you found out, will you?" I was just about to hang up.

"Sure. There's another address, if you're interested."

"Where?"

"It's another number, but the address it comes back to isn't anywhere near your place or Al's."

"Where, Calvin?" I was getting impatient.

"It's a place in Salt Lake. I wrote down the address. Just a second."

I could hear Calvin ruffling papers.

"You there?" he finally said.

"Yeah."

"According to the phone company, the number comes back to an address on Fort Union Boulevard."

CHAPTER 9

I dropped the phone and ran to my truck. Fort Union Boulevard was the address where Julianna was staying. I drove there with deliberate speed, a speed just short of reckless, my mind racing. I couldn't believe I'd been so naive, so blind. As I thought back, there was every indication that Hunt had infiltrated much deeper into my life than I realized. It wasn't just me he was watching—everyone in my life was in danger. I had to reach Julianna in time to make sure she was safe.

I pulled up to the house where Julianna was staying and got out of my truck. The house was quiet; there were no signs of a cop-killing maniac anywhere. I opened the screen door and knocked. After a several seconds (which seemed like minutes), a tall woman with dark, wet hair answered the door. For the second time that day, I was talking to a woman in her bathrobe.

The woman was obviously not pleased to be interrupted during her morning makeup and hairdo ritual. "Yes?" she said impatiently.

"Is Julianna here?" I asked.

"Oh, you must be Owen."

I nodded.

The woman tucked a lock of wet hair behind her ear. "She's not here."

"Where is she?"

The woman clearly didn't want to talk with me, but she answered anyway. "Julianna is gone."

"Gone?"

"She left this morning."

"Well, where did she go?" I asked.

"Home."

"*Home,* as in Kansas City home?

"Yes," she said. "Home."

My countenance must have registered complete defeat because the woman took pity on me and decided to provide more information. "She tried to call you last night but you weren't home. She tried this morning too," said the woman a bit accusingly. "She's been leaving you messages. The only flight she could get was early this morning. She left nearly an hour ago."

"Did she tell anyone she was going?"

"She told me. She would have told you if she could have reached you."

"I mean . . . did she use the phone?"

The woman must have sensed my apprehension and decided to frustrate me on purpose. "No, when she told me, she was standing right in front of me."

I stepped into the doorway, forcing Little Miss Annoying into the entry. I clenched my jaw and stared right into her beady eyes. "Did she say anything to anyone about this over the phone?"

"Yes," she said, stepping back a little. "She got the flight over the phone. She called a cab over the phone. She told her parents over the phone. You got something against phones?"

I didn't answer her; I was already running for my truck, kicking up snow as I went. I looked back as I drove away and saw the woman shaking her head and shutting the door.

I snaked ungracefully in and out of traffic on the freeway across the valley, hit an interchange, and headed west to the airport.

After one incredible near miss with a panel truck full of railroad workers, I decided that I didn't need to die trying to get to the airport and slowed down a little bit. I wasn't the most popular driver on the road that morning. Besides, slowing down gave me time to realize that having Julianna leave town was probably the best thing for her. I didn't need that kind of distraction while I was dealing with Hunt, and I could iron things out with Julianna later. Why I didn't just tell her I was getting baptized when I had the chance I'll never know. But now I just needed to make sure she got away safely. Hunt would know she was leaving, and I didn't want to take a chance that he would try to hurt her to get to me. I was comforted somewhat that the airport was crawling with armed guards these days. What could Hunt do at the airport?

I swerved carefully around several more cars on the freeway and took the Salt Lake City International Airport exit. I followed directions to the loading and unloading zone and, after agreeing to a cursory inspection of my vehicle, pulled to the curb and cut the engine.

I left my truck unattended and walked toward the doors to the ticket counters. A national guardsman in camouflage fatigues had his back to me, and I darted in the photoelectric doors before he turned around.

I didn't know what flight Julianna was booked on, but I assumed she would return, as she had come, on Delta Airlines. A closed-circuit television flashing flight numbers above my head showed a Delta flight to Kansas City leaving immediately at gate E15. I stood in the ticket line patiently until I was signaled to come forward by a tall, prim blond woman standing behind a desk stuffing ticket stubs into envelopes.

"Has the plane left? To Kansas City at E15?" I asked.

She looked at the screen of a computer snugly nestled behind the counter. "No," she said without emotion.

"Is there a way to get a message to the plane?"

"No," she said again. "Not unless this is an emergency. A real emergency," she added as an afterthought.

I wasn't in the mood to be pleasant, but I understood very well that my personal relationship needs wouldn't qualify as a real emergency to Delta Airlines and the Federal Aviation Administration. I wasn't going to be able to bluster my way past this woman, so I chose another tactic.

"I'm looking for someone. Julianna McCray? Can you tell me if she got on the flight?"

"No."

I wasn't getting on very well with Ms. Prim and Proper. I thought about (and decided against) crying to get what I wanted, but I had seen just about every other manipulation technique known to modern man in my years as a cop.

"Okay, I guess you probably aren't allowed to give out that kind of information."

"Exactly," she said without a smile.

I'd scored three syllables from Ms. Prim. It was time to go for the kill.

"I bet you could tell me if a knockdown, drop-dead, gorgeous redhead went through your gate."

Ms. Prim stood motionless behind the counter for several seconds, her face deadpan. "No, I couldn't."

I was just about to let out a mountainous sigh and give fake tears a try when Ms. Prim cracked a smile. "But I could tell you if someone like that *didn't* check on to that flight," she said.

"And? . . ." I said, grinning.

"I'm sorry, sir. No one like that picked up a ticket for that flight today. But there are a few no-shows."

"And when is the next one?"

Ms. Prim checked her log. "This evening."

I thanked Ms. Prim and decided to give her a new, nicer nickname if I ever ran into her again.

It looked like I had some breathing room. Julianna wasn't on the current flight. There was a good chance that she wasn't leaving until later. It was also possible that she decided not to leave at all and accounted for one of the no-shows. I could only hope. There was also as good a chance that Julianna had booked a flight on a different airline and was on her way home right now. It didn't matter—I wasn't going to find her there.

Remembering my truck parked in a tow-away zone, I made my way back to the exit. If I got a ticket, I'd pay. If I got towed, I'd have a private conniption and eventually pay to get my truck out of the impound lot. Those things were trivial right now.

I turned around in the ticket area and looked at the hundreds of people milling about or standing in lines, realizing I'd never find her in this mess even if she were here. I thought about calling her—if I only knew a number where I could reach her. I pulled my cell phone out of my pocket and saw a flashing envelope icon on the small screen. She'd left a message. Before I could thumb the numbers to access my voice mail, the phone rang. *Yes, it's Julianna,* I thought.

I pushed the talk button and said hello, expecting to hear the lovely lilt of Julianna's voice. Instead I heard the panicked whisper of a terrified Julianna.

"Owen . . . Owen!"

"Julianna!" I screamed into the phone, garnering stares from the people in the ticket lines.

Next I heard a male voice I recognized immediately—Raymond Hunt.

"There is no freedom from fear, Officer Richards." The line went dead.

"Julianna!" I screamed into the phone again. "Julianna!"

I got to the glass doors leading to the loading zone at a dead run and had to stop and wait for them to open slowly. I could see through the glass that there was a lot of activity around my truck. Several guardsmen with M16 rifles were standing around it, and one had a mirror on a long handle and was examining the underside.

There was only one car moving past us in the loading zone. It was a taxi, a yellow Ford Crown Victoria. The taxi drove slowly past my truck, the driver peering closely at the glass doors where I was standing. Everything about that face was familiar—it was Raymond Hunt's face. I could never forget it. He was scanning back and forth between my truck and the people milling around the loading zone. When his gaze hit me, my eyes locked on his sadistic smile.

The taxi lurched forward and sped up toward the airport exit lane. Through the back window I saw the horrified face of the woman I loved. It was Julianna—and Hunt had her.

* * *

I ran through the glass doors and sprinted toward my truck, digging in my fanny pack for my badge. I was holding it out toward an angry guardsman who was shouting commands at me and throwing his rifle up when a brilliant flash of light assaulted my eyes, driving them shut. A vicious rush of air threw me back against the building and was followed by an eerie, dull silence, as if all the sounds around the airport had been sucked violently into a vacuum. In another instant, I was sucked just as violently toward the street, and my badge was ripped from my hand by the unseen forces. The wind current was unbearable, and I couldn't catch my breath although I was gasping for air as hard as I could. When I opened my eyes again, I saw a ball of fire rising over a column of smoke. One of the guardsmen writhed on the ground in pain, trying helplessly to shield himself from the heat of the blast. As the dust cleared and my eyes adjusted, I made out the charred remains of my Dodge quad-cab pickup sitting in the loading zone.

I tried again to suck air into my burning lungs and got just enough oxygen to catch a breath. I was still unable to hear. I pulled myself upright against the building. I could see that my truck had blown up, but I was confused and hurt. What could have caused something like that?

I pushed myself away from the wall, still wondering what I'd done to cause such an explosion. There were people on the ground along the sidewalk, some obviously hurt and some just scared. My heart was racing, and my vision was still a little blurred.

I could hear a few dull noises now, but nothing distinct. A man in military fatigues holding a rifle stood in front of me and talked into my face, but all I heard was an uneven hum. There was still debris falling, some skittering on the cement and some floating in the air as if by levitation. I wasn't sure what was going on.

Running toward the street, I saw the speeding taxi pulling away. I put a hand out to steady myself on the burnt frame of my truck and burned the skin off my left palm. My own screaming sounded muffled. The man who had been talking to me tried to pull me back to the sidewalk, but I pushed him away into a stream of frightened witnesses and he was absorbed into the gathering crowd.

Only a few cars were parked sporadically along the loading zone. Most were occupied by dazed-looking passengers. I looked for a car that was empty and found nothing. Moving farther along the loading zone, I fought against a wave of people walking toward the explosion to get a closer look. Cops and national guardsmen with rifles at port arms were running in the direction of the blast trying to get everyone to stay back. There was mass confusion.

I finally saw what I wanted—a vehicle that was running. I climbed in, threw it in gear, and headed for the exit lane as fast as I could accelerate. The machine lugged and slowly built up speed. I slammed the accelerator against the floor but felt no surge of power, only an agonizingly slow acceleration. Of all the cars available at Salt Lake International, I had stolen a shuttle bus from the Marriott Hotel.

Hunt took the same freeway I'd come in on, which was now stacking up with traffic. Even under the best conditions, I could never hope to keep up with a Ford Crown Victoria, a car I knew a great deal about, as it was the very same model I drove every day at work. The shuttle bus just wasn't up to the task.

Hoping against hope, I pushed the accelerator against the floorboard, willing the bus on. Hunt was swerving through traffic gracefully ahead of me, and I tried to follow in his path. I struggled against the wheel to get the behemoth to go faster, and it gave in reluctantly each time I changed lanes. With a higher center of gravity, the bus rocked violently at each change of direction, and Hunt gained distance easily. The pressure in my ears was beginning to give way to a dull, nauseating ringing that was made worse by the sway of the bus. I clutched an ear and tried to dampen the noise, but that only made things worse.

I looked in the industrial-size rearview mirror installed over the dash and didn't recognize what I saw. My face was covered in soot and road oil thrown up in the explosion.

Some of what I considered to be incidental parts of my face, such as eyelashes and eyebrows, were partially singed along with select portions of my hair. *I never use those parts of my face anyway,* I thought.

My jacket sleeves had protected my arms, but my hands were slightly scorched. My wrists and fingers seemed to be operable, and I flexed them against considerable pain. I pulled a shard of torn metal from the cuff of my sleeve and threw it back into the passenger compartment.

The bus struggled over an overpass, and I saw my chance to gain speed on the downhill side. I already had my foot as far into the floorboards as I could sink it, so I took a firm grip and got ready to fight the wheel as I picked up speed.

"What's this?" said a sleepy voice behind me.

I looked over my shoulder to see a groggy male face framed with long, greasy blond hair.

"So, what is this?" he said again. He'd picked up the metal shard I'd thrown and was shoving it toward my face.

"What are you doing here?" I snapped.

"I'm taking a nap, dude. What're *you* doing here?" he responded insolently.

"This isn't your stop, Valley Boy. Now, get out of my way," I ordered. The boy was distracting me, and I tried to focus on the road and the traffic.

"Dude, what happened to you?" he said, looking at my burns. "Hey, this isn't the airport." He looked around at the traffic whizzing by.

"No kidding." I jerked the van to the side to avoid a nasty collision with a green Dodge minivan. Four angry family members had their faces in the windows glaring at me as I passed.

"Dude!" exclaimed my passenger.

"Quit saying that." Mr. Dude was, like, completely distracting.

"Alright," he said, apparently noting the rancor in my voice.

His voice sounded as though he were speaking through wax paper, and I could barely make out what he was saying through the resultant buzz. His reliance on the word *dude* was, however, just as irritating to my numbed ears as if he were screaming it at me—which he was.

"Dude, watch out!" he yelled.

I pulled the wheel sharply and slammed on the brake, narrowly avoiding the back end of a Simon Trucking tractor trailer. I decided to let my monosyllabic partner make his own vocabulary choices and focus on my driving. The yellow taxi was pulling farther ahead, tearing like a rocket eastbound on the freeway. I was moving steadily in that direction, but only as fast as the bus would take me. I rubbed some of the perspiration and soot off my forehead with the back of my arm and reestablished a solid grip on the wheel. Through the haze in my head, Dude was giving me directions.

"Left lane, left . . . go left."

I swerved left and saw several car lengths of freedom ahead of me. I stood on the accelerator and the bus stubbornly pushed forward.

I took directions from my new navigator and made steady headway toward Julianna, whose head I saw occasionally bobbing up and down in the distant taxi window.

My friend gave timely directions and saved us from certain death several times before he finally asked, "Dude, where're we going?"

"We're following that taxi," I said without explanation.

"Follow that cab," he laughed. "Uh, why?"

"Because," I said without thinking, "Raymond Hunt has the girl I love."

"Dude," said my friend. "It's a love thing. Awesome."

A loud screeching noise punctuated my friend's celebration, and it took a few moments for me to realize that I was hugging the lane divider a little too snugly, sending a shower of sparks into the median. The shuttle wasn't designed for this kind of abuse and shortly slowed to a dead stop, resting against the concrete barricade. She'd given me all she could.

I swung the door open and ran out onto the freeway. Traffic had come to a stop in the two inner lanes, and drivers were trying to change to the outside lanes to get around the smoking shuttle bus.

Eight powerful cylinders announced themselves just before it came into view. It was just what I wanted—a Vitamin C Orange, 1970 Plymouth Roadrunner in cherry condition, rumbling along in the fast lane looking for a place to merge right and get around my broken-down bus.

I ran out in front of the car and held my hands up. The driver, an irritated boy of about seventeen, reluctantly came to a stop and rolled down his window. I walked to the driver's side of the car and gave him a curt offer.

"I'll give you ten thousand dollars for your car."

"What?"

"Twenty," I said.

"Twenty? What?"

I thrust my arms into the window and got a good grip on his jacket. "Get out or I'll tear you into pieces and take you out through the wing window one chunk at a time!" I yelled.

"What's wrong with you?" he said, checking his blind spot and preparing to drive off.

By the time he'd spoken the last syllable, I had established a pretty good grip on his jacket and had him leaning out of the window to about his shoulders. My friend Dude put a stop to my madness. He was talking calmly into my ear and he had one hand on my shoulder.

"This ain't cool, dude," he was saying. Rational thought took over, and I stuffed the driver back into his window. Dude took over for me.

"You wanna see this bird fly?" Dude said to the boy. "For real, man. This is an emergency."

The driver was too confused to make a reasonable decision, and I had the door open and was in the driver's seat pushing him out of it before he knew what was going on. Dude got in the other side and our new friend was mashed up between us, still wide-eyed.

"You weren't really going to break this kid into chunks, were you, dude?"

"No, I just said that to simulate an atmosphere of cooperation," I said.

I put my foot on the clutch and gripped the Hurst pistol grip shifter.

"Four on the floor?" I asked the car's owner.

He smiled for the first time. "Yup. It's a 440 six-pack Superbird." He was obviously proud of his muscle car.

I let out the clutch, and the beast came to life. The taxi had a head start, but my new ride was just the ticket for a cruise up the freeway. The yellow Crown Victoria was mine.

Dude was apparently motivated by true love and gave excellent directions as I bobbed and weaved until we thought we saw a bit of yellow taxi up ahead. It was still eastbound, and when Interstate 80 started up Parley's Canyon toward Park City, it continued up the grade. Some of the slower cars started migrating toward the right-hand lanes, and I put my orange rocket in the fast lane and blew by a long string of cars. The taxi was trying to pass cars on the left-hand shoulder, but there wasn't enough room. Some of the cars ahead of us appeared to be getting tired of Hunt's aggressive driving and had him pinned into the fast lane behind a driver in a bronze Chevy Tahoe.

"Dude, we're making time!" I screamed as we charged up the hill.

My friend smiled at me from the copilot's seat and continued to shout orders. The owner of the car was starting to adjust to the new circumstances, and he smiled a little when he saw how much fun Dude and I were having driving with reckless abandon up the canyon.

"Far right, far right, man—I see daylight," the owner yelled, getting into the action.

The Plymouth lurched right and into an empty lane, where I made up nearly three car lengths on Hunt.

Hunt took the Park City exit and, in the lighter traffic, pulled almost out of view.

"Dude, give it some gas!" said my passenger.

I eased on the accelerator and felt another surge of power. *They don't make 'em like this anymore,* I thought.

I had gained a lot of ground and was just one car length behind the taxi now. I saw Julianna's head in the back window every once in a while, her red hair waving as the taxi bounced back and forth between lanes.

We were going well over the posted speed limit and ignoring all kinds of traffic-control devices. It was just a matter of time before a cop saw us, and that was just fine with me. I was ready for some help.

The last car between the taxi and me turned off, and I pulled up on Hunt's tail. He tried to outrun me, but his Crown Vic was no match for the Runner. I could see him looking back and forth at the cross streets, and I should have eased up, but I was too focused on catching up to him. I even thought about finding a place to run up alongside of him and ram him.

I was caught up in those thoughts when he suddenly jerked the wheel and plowed off onto a side street to my right.

My reflexes weren't quick enough, and I shot past the side street, Hunt running down it at full-bore.

It took me several hundred feet to stop the raging Roadrunner, and I didn't know Park City well enough to be aware of any side streets close by for me to parallel Hunt.

"Well, Mrs. Warneke," I said, "What would Jimmy Rockford do?"

"Who's Mrs. Warneke?" asked Dude.

"Hold on, Angel. We're coming around."

I jammed the Roadrunner in reverse and threw my right arm over the seat. All three of our heads went forward as I floored it and backed down the highway at full throttle, causing innocent drivers to swerve out of the way.

"Dude, what are you doing?"

"Rockford turn. Hold on."

"Who's Jimmy Rockford?" he screamed as the front end of the Runner flew around in an arc.

Almost all cops who work at night practice the famed Rockford turn, but few master it. Dude put his head down and covered his eyes as I forced the manual transmission into third gear against its will before our forward momentum ran out. I heard a nasty grinding noise come from underneath us, and the owner of the car cringed. Eventually the clunking in the transmission stopped, and we were racing back toward the cross street. I took the same turn as Hunt and accelerated through a new neighborhood development, but he was long gone.

We checked every side street without any luck and then decided to search for Hunt in Park City's historic downtown district.

"You guys look right," I ordered. "I'll look left." I couldn't believe it would be that easy to lose a yellow taxi in a place like Park City. There were only a couple of streets along historic Main Street and not very much real estate between them.

Dude had his head on a swivel, looking down each side street and through buildings for the yellow Crown Victoria. The owner of the Plymouth seemed worried that the transmission was going to fall out of the car. It sounded terrible whenever I changed gears.

"Not to worry," I told him. "It feels fine."

We made three trips up and down Main before heading back down the highway where we last saw Hunt.

"There, dude." My new friends were pointing up the hillside to a deserted gravel lot near a two-story, corrugated-steel building nestled against the mountainside. The building bore the Silver King Mine logo in faded black paint on its roof. The taxi sat in the gravel lot beside the small building, the back door standing ominously open. The car had been abandoned, and I knew where Julianna had been taken.

* * *

It wasn't difficult to find the entrance to the mine several hundred yards from the Silver King building. It had been well secured against Park City's curious and adventurous tourists, but Hunt had cut several links of chain and jimmied open a sliding steel door to gain access.

The main shaft had been dug over a number of years and took the form of one main vertical shaft with horizontal spurs leading out into the mountain at different angles, like branches off the trunk of a gigantic tree. I'd heard somewhere that some of the spurs were miles long and the main shaft could be over a thousand feet deep.

Access to the main tunnel was blocked by sturdy wooden panels held in place by large, square beams and anchored with bolts the size of my arm. By the looks of the roughly cut opening in the panels, Hunt had been here earlier with a reciprocating saw.

I peered down the mouth of the tunnel and saw pieces of dilapidated machinery cluttering the floor and two solid iron rails disappearing into the darkness.

Dude was following closely behind, looking over my shoulder.

"Go back to the car," I ordered. "Someone needs to take care of what's-his-name back there." The owner of the Roadrunner had wisely decided that the continued care of his car was more important than following two lunatics into a cave full of bats and trolls.

"But, dude."

"Back to the car."

He hesitated, a forlorn look in his eye as if I'd just canceled his trip to Disneyland.

I turned to face him and took him by the shoulders. "Look, this guy already killed my best friend. I'm not going to baby-sit you while he kills the only person left in the world that means anything to me."

"But . . ."

I intensified my grip on his shoulders and pulled his face toward mine. "Go back to the car," I said very softly, "before I kill you myself."

"Just trying to simulate an atmosphere of cooperation?" he asked.

Slowly I shook my head.

"I'll wait in the car." He turned on his heels and left.

I thought about following Dude out of the tunnel and going for real help. I could hear myself trying to explain this to the local police. Even I didn't believe it. As much as I wanted to charge into the blackness and save Julianna, I knew that was exactly what Hunt was counting on. Only a fool would go off half cocked like that.

"I'm not going to make it that easy for you, Raymond," I said softly. "Nothing in the world could draw me down that hole to you. Nothing."

"Owen!" I heard Julianna's scream echoing down the shaft. "Owen, help me!"

CHAPTER 10

The sound of Julianna's terrified screech from the darkness was like an ice pick being driven into my heart. With hands shaking from the sudden rush of adrenaline, I pawed my way deeper into the shaft. Despite the volume of Julianna's yell for help, I could tell that the scream had come from deep within the mine. Hunt wasn't lying in wait near the entrance; he was pulling a struggling Julianna deeper into the mountain. If I waited for help, Hunt would have time to lose himself somewhere deep inside. If I acted now, I could at least keep him on the move. I forged on, pistol now in hand.

The rocky floor was uneven and had pools of rank, stagnant water in places—not at all like the dusty rock I would have expected. Walking in a crouched position with my gun in front of me, I ran my left hand along the cool rock walls of the tunnel to orient myself in the blackness. The deeper I moved into the spur, the thicker the blackness became. After only a few hundred feet, the light from the entrance was merely a pinprick resembling a faint, sparkling star billions of miles from earth.

I'd spent most of my adult life working the night shift on the streets of Salt Lake, and though I was accustomed to the dark, this darkness was the real thing. There were no streetlights or stars, no neon signs or car headlights reflecting off streets and buildings. Nothing penetrated this blackness. I'd have to rely on my sense of hearing, which was temporarily diminished by the explosion at the airport.

I had a flashlight but wasn't able to use it without letting Hunt know just exactly where I was. I didn't know how he was armed, but I knew that if I turned on the light, one lucky shot in the direction of the beam would be enough to do me in. Good tactics dictated that I only use the light in short bursts coupled with sudden changes in direction. But from what I could feel, the terrain in the tunnel wasn't going to allow for that.

I strained to hear sounds ahead of me, but all I could make out was the noise of my own uneven footsteps splashing along the mine floor and echoing against the rock walls. I had to concentrate on each footfall to be quiet. Hunt would have the same concerns about noise that I did, even more so because he was dragging Julianna along with him.

I'd assumed that the spur was only as big as the entrance had been, about four feet wide and just over six feet tall, but when I felt in the darkness for the opposite wall on my right, I couldn't feel anything. I stepped over the uneven floor and racked my shin on something very hard. Reaching down, I felt two steel rails supported by rough, wooden ties running lengthwise in the tunnel. It was a narrow-gauge train track. If I had had one of those little ore carts, I would have zoomed down the tunnel and rescued Julianna like Indiana Jones. I wasn't Indiana Jones though; just what was I getting myself into?

The deeper I traveled into the emptiness, the more the oppressive weight of the mountain seemed to bear down on me—I could almost feel the raw tons of solid rock crushing down on my shoulders. Although I could move freely within the wide cavern, I had to suppress waves of claustrophobic panic and fear for Julianna by forcing my mind to focus on what I was doing.

Moving back to the left side of the tunnel so I could follow the wall, I pushed farther into the mountain. I stopped often to listen, hoping to hear something that would lead me to Julianna. Becoming more accustomed to the darkness, my senses became more acute and I could no longer hear ringing in my ears.

The water was now ankle deep in places and splashed as I walked. I groped my way back to the rails and stepped up on the slick iron railing, hoping to eliminate the noise by walking on them. Besides, my imagination was conjuring up images of mutant species of vermin, mammoth rats with sawlike buck-teeth and tails the size of pythons, wriggling through the murky water. The rails were just a bit too far apart to walk comfortably along, but out of the water I could travel more quietly, albeit slower.

I looked back, hoping to see the comforting tiny speck of light at the tunnel entrance, but it was gone and I no longer had any reference point within the blackness. I'd read somewhere about the human nervous system's ability to sense its own position in space through electrical impulses—proprioceptors—located at nerve endings. Mine must have been slightly out of adjustment because I was experiencing a slight case of vertigo, and I fell off the iron rails often, each time making a tremendous noise. My shins also took a beating on the rails and wooden beams. On one fall, something sharp drove itself into the palm of my left hand, causing me to drop my flashlight. I spent several panicked minutes fishing for it in the water. When I found it, I let out a long sigh, unaware that I'd been holding my breath.

I could feel the sting of the injury to my palm, but I couldn't see anything. I thought about my predicament and decided that, under these conditions, stealth was more important than speed, so I continued my laborious shuffle along the iron rails.

I stopped often to listen for sounds indicating movement in front of me. It was the only tactical wisdom I had practiced all day other than keeping the flashlight off. I still had a tremendous urge to turn it on and illuminate the whole tunnel, but I knew that kind of blunder was suicide. Hunt would have me in his sights before I could get a good look around.

The only impetus to go forward was the thought of Julianna alone with Hunt in the dark. Emboldened by that thought, I pushed farther and farther into the darkness until I finally heard what I'd been waiting for—a faint, splashing sound ahead, not far away.

I froze stock-still, balancing on the iron rails. My body tensed and my legs quivered from exertion, but I dared not move—not until I heard another noise to orient me to their exact location. I listened for what seemed like forever, feeling my lungs heaving and my heart pounding in my eardrums. Under intense pressure, those two sounds always seemed louder than they really were.

After some time, I heard the trickling of water. Was that all it was? Was I mistaking the sound of an underground spring for the sounds of human movement?

My thighs were fatigued from balancing on the rails, so I stepped down to straighten up and stretch. I was feeling for the wall with my outstretched hand when I saw a brilliant muzzle flash and heard the deafening concussion of a pistol shot. I couldn't fire back down the tunnel without risking Julianna's life, so I dove to the right, expecting to hit solid rock. I felt nothing as I rolled past where I'd imagined the wall to be and fell into a side tunnel leading off the main spur

I'd been walking down. No other circumstance could have been more fortuitous—or more debilitating. I was behind cover, but I was also pinned down. If Hunt had a flashlight of his own, he could turn it on and create a curtain of light that I couldn't see past. From a position behind the light source, he could move freely and see everything in my end of the tunnel. He'd have me pinned down for good.

The use of a curtain of light was a basic patrol tactic that all cops used to their advantage when they could. By aiming a spotlight into the rearview mirror of a stopped car, they could establish concealment behind a wall of light. I didn't know if Hunt was aware of the old curtain of light trick, but if he was, I had to beat him to the punch.

I crawled forward into the main tunnel and reached out in the darkness for the nearest rail. I set my flashlight on a railroad tie about a body length behind the small side spur where I'd landed when I fell. When I turned it on, I wanted the flashlight to illuminate the side spur and draw Hunt's fire.

After the flashlight was in place, I moved to the side of the tunnel opposite the side spur and took a prone position. I wiped off my sweaty hands and took a firm grip on my pistol. Half submerged in the water, I reached for the flashlight. Taking a deep breath, I turned it on. Hundreds of feet of rock wall were suddenly illuminated. Raymond Hunt was standing dead center in the tunnel about forty yards ahead of me, engaged in a silent struggle with Julianna. He looked up with angry red eyes and raised his pistol to fire. I would have ended it right there except that Julianna was between us. Hunt reached around her and fired a series of rounds, aiming toward the side spur, a natural defensive position that attracted his attention. The bullets ricocheted around me, some whining down the tunnel, others crashing into the walls and pelting me with shattered rock.

I held my fire so as not to endanger Julianna. Forty yards was a long shot with a pistol. Luckily, Hunt couldn't see past the light and continued to shoot toward the other side of the tunnel. I kept my pistol up and on target as Julianna struggled to break free. Hunt would have to expose himself sooner or later.

She was screaming my name now each time Hunt shot. He changed his aim, desperate to extinguish the dull glow that illuminated him, and I could tell he was well trained and disciplined, shooting only a round or two at a time in a slow, uneven cadence. But he only had the slimmest chance of hitting the flashlight at the distance he was at. I had only to hunker down and await my opportunity, hoping that a lucky shot wouldn't put an end to me.

The interior of the tunnel glowed an eerie gray. The roof and walls were mainly dry and dusty, unlike the floor. The ore cart rails made straight lines that extended into the darkness beyond the power of my flashlight. In places, the walls were reinforced with iron and wooden beams. Many of the beams were rotted, and jagged, iron spikes protruded from them.

Hunt was still struggling with Julianna, pausing occasionally to spatter me with rock chips. I couldn't tell what the hang-up was, but it appeared that Julianna was either stuck or had purposely wedged her legs around the ore cart rails to slow Hunt down. Either way, I could see his frustration mounting, and I realized that sooner or later he'd give up, shoot Julianna, and make a run for it.

Every nerve and muscle fiber in my body screamed for me to rush Hunt, pistol belching flame and forehead sweating raindrops like a B-movie hero. But I had to wait for my opportunity.

Hunt was pulling harder now on Julianna's leg, and I could hear him cursing her through clenched teeth. He was getting more and more aggravated as the moments passed.

"Stop, I can't!" I heard Julianna sobbing, "Stop! You're breaking my leg!" I couldn't bear to hear her wailing like that; opportunity or not, I had to do something.

I raised up into a sprinter's stance, preparing to charge, and that's when I saw it. She was sending me a signal, clear and meaningful. The four fingers of her right hand were extended against the soiled leg of her pants, her thumb purposefully hidden behind her palm. Julianna was code four. She was toying with him, and she wanted me to know it. *That's my girl,* I thought, *Now, don't push him too far.*

This was my opportunity. Crawling low over the rails, I reached the flashlight and turned it off. The tunnel turned black again, even blacker than before, if that was possible. Then, I moved in a controlled rush forward down the tunnel. Hunt emptied his pistol down the long black corridor, round after round spitting from his pistol and tumbling along the rock walls. I felt a small tug under my left arm and instinctively pulled my shoulder down snugly. I could feel the warmth of blood, but it didn't hurt. I'd been shot right where Lewis had been shot—and by the same man.

I heard the click of the slide on Hunt's pistol lock back. He was out of ammo. Whether he was reloading or not I couldn't tell. Hugging the left wall, I stepped quickly, pistol up and with deliberate, controlled speed toward where I'd last seen the murderer of my best friend.

Julianna was wailing now, covering the noise I was making and drawing me to her. It was a deadly game of blind man's bluff.

Another barrage of gunfire filled the cavern from farther down the tunnel, and instinctively I fired two aimed rounds at the muzzle flash, hoping that Hunt had abandoned Julianna and moved away in response to my attack. As I walked in the blackness, a shard of timber sticking out from the wall sliced my cheekbone.

I winced and swiped at the sharp pain in my face with the back of my hand, never losing my focus on the blackness in front of me. I quickly flashed my light on and saw Julianna alone only several yards away. I couldn't see Hunt. Julianna had wedged her foot between an iron rail and one of the decaying wooden beams to slow Hunt down, but she easily freed herself and limped toward me.

"Are you hurt?" I asked, turning the flashlight off and reaching out for her.

"I'm okay, but I think you hit Hunt."

"Good. Let's get you out of here."

I held onto her jacket, pushing her ahead of me as we hugged the walls and made our way out the way we'd come. There was no telling what kind of maze we were in, and I was wary of Hunt circling back and somehow getting in front of us for a slaughter. We had to get out fast.

Julianna was a tough girl, but the injury to her leg was slowing us down.

"Ju, we have to move faster. Here, I'm going to carry you." I ducked under her shoulder and lifted her to my back. Within minutes we spotted a small shaft of natural light ahead of us and began to breathe easier.

At the shaft entrance, the light was so bright to our eyes that we both had to squint, even though the sky was dark and overcast.

I stepped out of the mine shaft still carrying Julianna on my back. The orange Roadrunner was long gone, but the taxi was still sitting in the gravel lot with its door open. I set Julianna in the front seat; the keys were still in the ignition.

"You take the taxi. See if you can find some help."

"Owen, your face."

I rolled my eyes. "Just go get some help."

"You're not going back in there! Your face—it looks awful. There's a big flap of skin torn off and . . ." She gasped.

"Owen, under your arm, you're bleeding . . . let me see." She pulled at my shredded jacket to reveal a glistening, crimson stain along my ribs. Parts of my shirt had congealed in the wound, and it was difficult to see how much damage had been done. Julianna probed the injury carefully, pulling away layers of cloth.

I winced. "You have to go Ju; I'll be okay."

"No," she said. "Get in the car. I'll drive."

I didn't say anything, but I didn't get in the car.

"Owen, you can't go back in there. You're acting crazy," she said.

"Julianna," I said, "I'm not crazy. I was beginning to think I was, but I'm not. I'm not going to lose Hunt this time."

Julianna's mouth was gaping. "Owen, listen to me. Read my lips. You are hurt. Let the authorities handle this."

"Ju, I am the authorities—no, I'm *the* authority."

Julianna turned her head away.

I touched her cheek, and she turned her head toward me. "The man destroyed my truck, tarnished my reputation beyond repair, dragged the woman I love through half a mountain . . . and, worst of all, Julianna McCray—are you listening?"

She still wouldn't look at me.

"Worst of all, Raymond Hunt took my authentic trident Mariner's hat."

That brought her face around. "You can't really mean that," she said.

"What, that I love you?" I looked in Julianna's deep green eyes. "Well, I do. I've been in love with you for a long time now, and . . ."

"No, you dolt. Are you really going to risk your life for a stupid Mariner's hat?"

* * *

I left Julianna slack jawed, sitting in the front seat of the taxi. She wasn't at all happy with my decision to go back after Hunt, but she hadn't slapped me when I told her again that I loved her. I was willing to claim any small victory at this point.

I entered the mine and traveled in the darkness, which wasn't as oppressive this time. Using my flashlight in short bursts to orient myself, I followed the tunnel to where I'd last seen Hunt. I illuminated the area momentarily, looking for fresh blood. Julianna said he'd been hit, and the amount of blood would give me critical information about Hunt's physical condition. However, there was no sign of it. As soon as I snapped the light off, I crossed to the other side of the tunnel and moved forward, stepping carefully and stopping to listen.

I fought the impulse to charge ahead. When I hit water, I stepped back up on the rails and moved at a painstakingly slow pace. The initial adrenaline rush which numbed my injuries was wearing off; each step was becoming a labor, and each breath a formidable task. My side had broken open and was bleeding steadily again. My face, too, was bothering me, and I found it hard to concentrate on what I was doing. Doubts entered my mind, and a sickening feeling enveloped me. Something wasn't right. I stepped off the rails onto dry ground and leaned against the wall, praying silently that I would make it out of this alive. I slowly lowered myself to the floor and knelt, listening to the silence. There was nothing for a long time.

"I know you're down there, Richards." The cold, calloused voice startled me out of a dull stupor. It came from deep in the tunnel, where Hunt had been lying in ambush.

I didn't respond.

"I know you're there, somewhere. I can feel you." He wanted me to make a sound so he could shoot me. I slowly raised my gun and pointed it in the direction of Hunt's voice. The first of us to get a good fix on the other was going to win this battle.

"It's a pity you won't live long enough to see what I'll do to the people you love." Hunt spat his parting shot at me like poison.

I only need to live long enough to take you out, I thought. I aimed at the sound of his voice and pulled the trigger. In the muzzle flash I could see that I was off target. Hunt returned fire, shooting a round that ricocheted down the tunnel behind me. I sprawled out on the ground and prepared to take another shot when Hunt ran farther into the tunnel and I heard his feet scuffing across the uneven floor. I lunged to my feet and followed the sound of him around a slight bend, watching the silhouette of his body pass in front of a shaft of hazy light just before he disappeared around another corner.

The light up ahead was a welcome sight, and I charged forward, stopping only long enough to navigate the sharp bend in the tunnel with tactical care. Once I was sure Hunt wasn't hiding just around the bend, I moved again.

The glow ahead of me was getting brighter, and as I rounded another corner a blinding shaft of light assaulted my eyes. I squinted and saw Hunt struggling up a steep bank of boulders toward daylight. I stopped, took aim, and pulled the trigger of my pistol twice, then again. I was too late, and Hunt disappeared out of a hole he'd dug in the tunnel ceiling.

I ran for the exit, slipping on the loose rocks on the mine floor. Before I'd made it halfway up the embankment toward the outside, a small dark, object dropped into the tunnel from outside and I heard the distinctive tinny sound of a grenade spoon hitting rock. I felt the stiff concussion of the explosion before I saw anything. It seemed to hit me from all sides at once—a violent explosion that shook the earth.

The roof above me gave way abruptly, and I felt myself falling to the floor under a barrage of rocks. The walls closed in, pulverizing me as I was forced under the weight of the rocks and dirt. I pulled against the current of rocks, forcing my arms forward and churning with my legs.

I felt a stab of pain in my lower back. A rush of warm air passed above me as the first hot shock wave of the explosion traveled down the tunnel. The vacuum effect of the blast sucked the air away, and I struggled for breath. I filled my lungs, but there was no precious oxygen. I tried again, stars flying before my eyes. Nothing. I inhaled again, still struggling for air. My last thought was of Julianna's red, waving hair and graceful, slender fingers reaching out for me, and then there was nothing.

CHAPTER 11

When I realized I could breathe again, I slowly struggled to open my eyes through the dust and film that covered my face. I might have thought I was dead, but I intuitively knew that dead people didn't feel this much pain. I was alive all right. No doubt about it. The next, most important question was, would I soon be dead?

After some spastic blinking, I was able to hold my eyes open but found it made no difference in the unmitigated blackness. However, there was air now and I could feel my arms and legs a little. I was still wedged in the rubble, but I could tell there was some space around me. I wondered how much oxygen was available and how long it was going to take for me to die. I doubted I was in any more danger from Raymond Hunt. He wasn't coming back into the mine, where he undoubtedly thought I had died in his little explosion.

I should have known, or at least anticipated, that Hunt would booby-trap the mine. After what he'd done to my beloved truck, what else should I have expected?

As I regained consciousness, I began to panic. I'd never been fond of small places, but under this mass of rocks, I couldn't move at all. When I tried to take a deep breath, I found that I couldn't move my diaphragm against the pressure of the earth around me. I was truly buried alive.

Raymond Hunt was no longer my main concern. In fact, my perspective on life had changed dramatically in those few moments while reality dawned on me. There were more important things in life, or there had been. A string of those important things ran through my mind as I lay there, struggling to breathe. How would my family feel after this? I loved them much more than I'd ever shown them. I was close to my sister in Seattle, but I hardly ever called to show care or concern about her life. I loved my parents too, but I was miserable at maintaining that relationship. It occurred to me that I wasn't a very good brother or son.

I'd heard that people who were about to die saw their lives pass before them. At that moment, I felt like one of those people, and while the life-passing-before-me thing wasn't entirely true, there wasn't very much else to think about. I hadn't been a bad person, but I had certainly let a lot of opportunities slip by. I could have made a bigger difference in the lives of some of the people I knew. I had a truckload of regrets.

I struggled against the pressure again, just to see if I could make some forward progress. I couldn't, leaving me to guess where in the tunnel I was and how far under I was buried. I had no idea.

I wriggled slightly and felt some of the rubble move around my body. Would one wrong move bring the mountain down on me and squish me like a bug? It was decision time. I could move and possibly let the rocks and boulders crush the life out of me quickly and painfully, or I could remain as still as a stick and let hunger and lack of oxygen kill me slowly and agonizingly. I thought about that option for a long time. It was like finally getting your chance on *Let's Make a Deal* and knowing there was a booby-trap prize behind each door.

"I'll take door number three, Monte. If it's all the same to you." Just the breathing required to rasp out a sound caused the earth to tighten around me, and I got a mouthful of dust for my trouble.

It wasn't going to do me a tremendous load of good to sit and stew about my situation, so I did my best to come up with a logical plan for trying to dig myself out. Because I was pinned in what seemed like the center of the earth and could move each appendage only so far, my choices were severely limited. I knew I wanted to go up, so that formed the foundation for my plan.

With that in mind, I made a half-hearted effort to push down with my arms and legs. As expected, the rocks and debris around me shifted, and I couldn't tell if I moved up or the mountain moved down. In fact, I started thinking about people buried in avalanches and how they can't really tell up from down. I wondered which way I was actually oriented.

An empirical test wasn't going to be as easy as it had been for Sir Isaac Newton; he had apples and trees to work with. Yet after a few moments, my solution was obvious. In the darkness, I had absolutely no need for my eyes right then, and if my situation didn't change soon, I'd have no need for them at all, so I decided to sacrifice them for the cause.

I opened my eyes and moved my right arm, which happened to be pinned over my head. I figured, if dust fell into my eyes, I was going to dig in the direction it came from and assume I was headed away from the center of the earth—toward freedom. I tried it, and nothing much happened except I felt the movement of small particles of rock trickling past my face.

I tucked my chin down, inhaled, and then exhaled to get some dust moving. Again, nothing fell into my eyes. I was able to move my head in the direction of my left armpit and then tried to move my left arm. I was immediately rewarded with paroxysmal blinking and a fair amount of eyeball discomfort.

The evidence suggested that I was actually lying on my right side, with most of the mountain under me. On a day of limited successes, this was a big morale booster. If nothing else, I'd managed to fill the last few hours of my life with an industrious project, and I now knew which way was up.

I now had something to work for. I began to wriggle in the direction of my left arm. The mountain squeezed and released as I went, and I sensed some slow movement upward, maybe a few inches.

Time was another unknown. I didn't really know how long I'd been pinned under the debris. It could have been minutes or hours, and while it didn't seem all that important, for some reason I wanted to know what time it was. If I lived, my watch and I could do a Timex commercial, claiming, "it took a licking and kept on ticking." I didn't even know if I was still wearing a watch though, because I couldn't feel it.

For that matter, I wondered what had become of my pistol. It, too, had become part of the mountain. My flashlight was still gripped firmly in my left hand, but other than that all I had was my quick wit.

Quick wit? Why hadn't I lost some of that from lack of oxygen? Maybe I wasn't buried very deep after all and some oxygen *was* getting to me. The thought gave me hope, and the hope gave me the will to strive harder to free myself.

I squirmed some more. At times the rocks settled around me so tightly that I thought I could no longer move, while at other times I encountered great success and the rocks seemed almost loose.

I don't know how long it took or how many times I struggled and then gave up, but eventually my left hand, still holding the flashlight, emerged into what felt like a great open space. Most of the rocks I had to move were small, less than the size of grapefruits, but a few were much larger.

I dug quite slowly and methodically until I finally reached the surface of the rocks and emerged into what had to be a section of old tunnel. The explosion had sealed Hunt's makeshift exit and collapsed at least a part of the tunnel behind me, but there was a good chance that most of the mine was still intact.

I clicked on my flashlight and found that my new prison was a piece of tunnel about twenty feet in length and over eight feet high. The walls of the tunnel were just wider than my outstretched arms. There were no iron rails along the floor, but I managed to find two pieces of what I presumed were rail spikes.

I rested a few a minutes in my new home, taking the opportunity to stretch out on the damp floor. I looked at my wrist, noticing I was still wearing my watch. Unfortunately, it was crunched, so I couldn't tell how long I'd been in the mine. No Timex endorsements here. The licking was just too much for it. Like it really mattered at this point.

I assessed my injuries again, but not much had changed. My side was still bleeding, and the flap of skin that had been hanging on my face was still flapping. My entire body was one large contusion.

Yet none of that made any difference unless I was able to free myself. Escape didn't appear likely, as the rocks at either end of the tunnel were much larger than the ones I'd freed myself from. Many of them were too large to move. All I'd accomplished so far was to find a bigger tomb. But it was either dig or perish, so I chose the former.

I started as far up as I could reach, up next to the ceiling, and began to pull rocks down. In an effort to save battery life, I shut the flashlight off while unearthing myself and managed to beat my legs to death with falling debris. Eventually a pattern developed. I'd dig until I could no longer move rocks because they were too large, and then I'd move to a new location with the aid of my flashlight.

I rested often and sometimes thought I was running out of air only to find that I was merely winded from exertion. I wondered if air was getting into the tunnel through the rocks and decided to find out by pointing the flashlight at the rubble at the end of the tunnel and dropping handfuls of dust in front of some of the larger spaces between rocks. As the dust fell in the beam of the light, I could see evidence of small air currents in the movement of the dust particles. It was good news and bad. I was going to be able to breathe, and so, it was going to take me longer to die. Actually, what it really meant was that I was probably trapped very close to the surface of the mountain. That was, yet again, good news and bad.

When I ran out of places to dig, I'd stop, sit down, and resign myself to that slow boring death I'd feared from the beginning. Then, with renewed vigor, I'd attack a new section of the rock wall. There seemed to be no other solution.

My flashlight was beginning to fade, the batteries slowly surrendering, so I shut it off. I moved several more small rocks near the ceiling of the tunnel and felt what I initially thought was a reinforcing beam. I dug around it with one of my iron spikes and felt it break free. I took the object to the floor and turned on the flashlight. It wasn't a chunk of wooden beam after all, and in the dim glow of my waning flashlight, I could see the object was a wooden box about the size of a small ice chest.

I dragged the box onto the floor and examined it. An iron hasp, heavily corroded, secured the lid, but it opened easily under the pressure of my iron spike. I lifted the lid to find a collection of different sized, rough papers.

Most of the papers were written on, and I had to strain to read with my dim light. Lists of names with dates and places indicated I had found some sort of family history records. And there were pictures—charcoal drawings of men and women, landscapes and animals. I shuffled through them, noticing that they were all signed and dated. One picture in particular jumped out at me. It was a simple drawing of a man posing in front of a backdrop of tents and makeshift dwellings. The image's likeness to the subject was a testament to the talent of the artist, right down to the zippered fanny pack—I should know; the picture was of me. These were Lem LeJeune's family records, over a century and a half old.

I stared at the pictures, using up what was left of the batteries in my flashlight until the room became dark. Then, by feeling around, I placed the papers back in the box and fastened the rusty latch.

I was feeling lousy and really beginning to hurt, so I ripped several inches off of the bottom part of my shirt and wrapped it tightly around my torso in a vain effort to stem the slow flow of blood from the wound in my side. Then I sat quietly, somewhat reclined, with my eyes closed and my head resting on the boxful of forgotten memories. I don't know how long I sat there thinking of Lem and his adoptive grandfather, Bart LeJeune.

I'd been blessed to know both of them. In fact, I realized in the dark my whole life had been a blessing. I was sorry that it would end so soon, but there was very little I could do about that now. I wondered if just wanting to get baptized would help my case in the afterlife. Death, which seemed so near, was not that frightening . . . only disappointing.

I shifted my sore and tired body. Standing, I stretched my limbs and worked out the kinks. Then I sat back down against the wall. My thoughts now turned to Hunt. I'd done what I could to slow him down. Maybe he would even die of his injuries. Strangely, I wanted him to be alive. I wanted him to have to stand accountable for what he'd done. Then again, either way he'd be accountable.

What about Julianna? Would she commiserate with Etta over my death? She would likely move on and marry a man strong in his religion. If he didn't take his religion seriously, I'd visit him from beyond the grave and change his mind. The thought was ridiculous, but it seemed rational enough given my situation.

I considered all that for a while, and then my thoughts turned back to the box. I sat against the tunnel wall and pulled the wooden chest closer to me, wrapping my arm around it. If anyone ever found my body, I wanted the box found too. Lem LeJeune and his ancestors deserved that much.

The image of Bart LeJeune, the French-Canadian lumberman turned soldier whom I'd come to know during my strange episode in the Missouri backwoods, suddenly came to mind. My memory of him was so vivid; I could almost see him standing there in the darkness of the tunnel among the musty rubble and rock. He was tall and rugged, with an ornate, silvering moustache. He always wore a wide-brimmed fedora hat low over his eyes and cocked slightly sideways and a black canvas duster that hung below his knees.

It was comforting to imagine just one familiar face there in the tunnel to see me past the portal of death. And then, Lewis's image came to mind just as vividly. Lewis was such a friendly, strong person. I remembered his tall, tan, athletic frame and his neatly trimmed dark hair. I could picture him smiling at me, his sea-foam green eyes shining.

I shut my eyes, wondering if I was dying. I knew family members and friends would be waiting to meet me upon my death, but where was the light everyone always spoke of? There was supposed to be a light when you died. Feeling weak and drained in the blackness, I lifted my arm and gingerly pressed on my side. Pain shot through by chest, leaving me momentarily nauseated. Was I hallucinating? I rubbed my hand over my face and eyes and then opened my eyes again. Lewis's and LeJeune's energy and presence were still there.

"I don't want to die," I whimpered.

Owen, fear not. Reason with the Lord, my mind heard. It was Bart's unique French accent. I stopped moving and listened for another sound. Maybe I was crazy. Maybe the oxygen was running out. Maybe it was a desperate subconscious suggestion. My heart told me it was more than that. Again, I felt it. *Reason with the Lord. What do you really want, Owen?*

What did I really want? I wanted to talk with my parents one last time. I wanted to call my sister in Seattle. I wanted to see one more sunrise over the Wasatch Mountains. I wanted to spend the rest of eternity loving Julianna.

I held on more tightly to the box, reaching to my chest with one hand and touching my Message From Home card through my jacket. I could feel the faint outline through the fabric. I was supposed to write my baptismal date on that card, but I hadn't. Fear, stubbornness, and independence had kept me from doing it. But now what? Would I die alone in the dark and have to wait with those whose names were written on the pages in the box I clutched tightly?

Reason with the Lord. The thought came to my mind again.

"You know I'm not good at waiting. I will not just sit here and wait to die."

I pushed myself to my feet and felt my way around the rock blocking the tunnel. I pulled at the large rocks, trying to get one to move just a few inches in the hopes that it would, in turn, loosen another rock, and then another. The process was slow and tedious, and I dug and scraped, dislodging small pieces of rock, until the ends of my fingers were raw. Every once in a while, I'd manage to move a few rocks. Then I hit a roadblock—a boulder the size of a Volkswagen Beetle. I pulled again and again, even resorting to sitting on the ground and pushing with my legs, but nothing in the rock pile would move. I climbed up onto the rock and braced myself against the ceiling, trying to get some leverage, and pushed with all of the strength my legs could muster. It was no use. The mountain would not move. I dropped slowly to my knees in a defeated slump.

You're pushing with the wrong muscles, Owen. It was Lewis's voice. I relaxed and leaned against the giant rock, tears forming in my eyes from the pain in my body as well as from the reality of my ultimate fate. "I can't move this rock myself," I whispered.

Have faith, Owen. Our prayers are with you, and we are many.

"Please," I said softly, "please. I admit it. I can't do this by myself. I'm ready for help now. It's not like I expect an army of angels riding chariots of fire to swoop down and rescue me. I just want to live long enough to be baptized. Please, Father in Heaven . . ." I poured out my soul in prayer, and then sat in the still darkness as an overwhelming feeling of peace washed over me. It was that same feeling I'd experienced when the little girl at Lewis's funeral had borne her testimony. It was that awesome burning that left me breathless, my chest and throat aching. Only this time, I knew what it was.

I felt a clear and urgent prompting to move the box and myself. I obeyed immediately, hefting the box to my hip, then feeling my way quickly to the far side of the tunnel, where I set the box on the floor. The ground began to shake, and a loud roar filled the confines of my tomb. A sudden shot of adrenaline pulsed through me, yet I felt a strange sense of security and calmness. Earth and rocks began to fall from the ceiling of the tunnel and fill the room with dust. Even though I couldn't see, I squeezed my eyes shut and buried my face in my arms. My mouth filled with dirt and dust, and I could feel the grit between my teeth as rocks collided around me.

The rocks eventually settled, and light penetrated the darkness. I blinked spastically, trying to adjust my eyes to the sudden brightness coming from above, and breathed in as much fresh air as my lungs would allow.

Thousands of pounds of earth, rocks, and snow from the ceiling had given way and covered the tunnel floor where, moments before, I'd been kneeling. I could still hear a thundering noise coming from outside, so I didn't hesitate to sprint up the loose rock and out a gaping hole in the ceiling of the mine. Even in my diminished physical condition, I made the climb easily.

I stopped halfway up and looked back into the blackness. The box. I climbed back into the hole and clawed for it in the debris. I found it and held it to my chest as I made my way back up to the exit. The dust particles suspended in the filtering sunlight began to pulse in rhythm with the noise coming from outside. I peered slowly through the hole and saw, suspended above me, a fleet of matte black helicopters, beating the air with their rotors.

"Unbelievable," I said, shaking my head and climbing from the gaping cavity in the earth. Upon reaching the surface, I could scarcely see because of the bright sunlight reflecting off the snow and the wind created by the helicopters' rotors. I wiped my watering eyes on my sleeve and waited out the swirling snow as the helicopters moved off.

I had imagined myself deep in the mountain, but glancing back I realized I'd been buried only ten or fifteen feet under the surface. From where I was standing, I could see Park City and the valley below. In fact, I wasn't far from the entrance to the Silver King mine.

The helicopters thrummed in the distance as I made my way down the mountain. I saw people climbing the hill just ahead, pistols and rifles at the ready. As they got nearer I recognized their uniforms; they were Park City police officers.

"Get your hands up! Hands up!" yelled one of the nearest officers.

I carefully placed the box on the ground and complied with the officers' orders. I was made to lie down and keep my hands out. The makeshift bandage around my side had long since become useless, and the blood soaked through my jacket onto the snow.

"That's enough, that's enough." I recognized the New York accent. Lem LeJeune was running to my rescue. "That's enough; let him up," the FBI agent ordered.

I rolled over on my side and gave LeJeune a grin. "Oh brother, two LeJeunes in one lifetime is about more than I can handle."

"What? Where's Hunt?"

I shrugged as best I could, considering my injuries. "He got out just before the tunnel collapsed."

"From the same place as you?"

"I think so," I said. "Not far from here."

LeJeune gave a series of commands into a radio and then looked at me, for the first time seeing my condition. "You look like . . . you look awful."

"Thanks, I've had better days. Did Julianna reach you?"

"Where is she? How did you know where to find me?"

"Whoa, slow down, pal. First of all, Julianna's doing great. She has a broken ankle, but she's fine. Calvin, you know, the neighbor kid—he's the one who saved your bacon. The kid's a prodigy with computers. He told Al about the modem on your phone line and broke about a half dozen federal laws getting us Hunt's address on a silver platter.

"We raided an apartment a half a block from your place and found all of Hunt's research on you. I was down at the airport picking through your truck when I got word of a small explosion on the ski slope. Being the great detective that I am, I figured you were up here spoiling my perfect record at the Olympics."

"But how did you get here so fast?"

He smiled again. "I came by chariot, of course." LeJeune turned and gestured to the sky. "Chariots of fire in the sky."

The formation of six Blackhawk helicopters was at full tilt, screaming up the canyon over Park City, which explained the great noise I'd heard from the tunnel.

LeJeune's arm swept over his head in a grand gesture toward the sky. He gave me a serious look. "If they don't find Hunt, no one will."

"Why did you say that?" I asked.

"Because . . . these guys are good."

"No—the part about the chariots of fire?"

LeJeune looked perplexed. "Give me a break, plowboy. It's just a figure of speech." LeJeune shook his head. "Oh brother. Westerners."

I remembered the box. "Oh, I got this for you." I pointed to it on the ground.

"What is it?"

"What does it look like? It's a box." It was my turn to shake my head. "Easterners."

LeJeune bent over and picked it up. "Evidence or something? What is it?"

"You'll find out later. Where's Al now?"

"I don't know. He said to tell you he's got your back."

"We need to find him."

LeJeune shook his head. "You don't look so good. Are you sure you're okay?"

"Let's go."

LeJeune made a couple of inquiries into his radio, then hoisted the box onto his shoulder. We started the hike down the hillside toward the golf course, LeJeune tromping along with the box and me limping beside him.

"There should be a car waiting somewhere on the front nine," he said.

LeJeune's government SUV, a blacked-out Chevrolet Suburban, sat on a smooth, snowy expanse of what was probably a green of the Park City Municipal Golf Course. As we approached, LeJeune gave the driver the signal to start it up, and the engine turned over. I limped toward the back door of the vehicle and started to climb in, but LeJeune stopped me.

"You're not going die or something, are you? Not in my rig."

I shook my head and struggled into the open door. "Do you care if I get the seat a little bloody?"

"No problem; it's a company ride. As long as you live, I don't care how messy it gets."

The truck lurched forward and bounced over the landscape, leaving the Park City cops to fend for themselves. As we made our way off the course and onto the road, I rolled down the window and watched as the Blackhawks unloaded their human cargo. My first glimpse of the elusive United States' antiterrorist team was incredible. Men in white and black camo were fast roping out of the six Blackhawks hovering over the trees high up the mountainside.

"You ever do that?" I asked LeJeune.

"Fast rope? Sure," he said. "I swallow swords and belch flames too. What do you think I am, an idiot?"

"Just wondered." I turned my face away from him and grimaced, letting LeJeune talk and hoping that he wouldn't realize the extent of my injuries and send me to the hospital.

"You SWAT dogs are all alike. Actually, I was going to take a class in fast roping at the FBI academy. The instructor got me up in the bird and facing the rope, see. 'Hey,' I said, 'I get no instructions?' He said, 'Sure, there's the rope and there's the ground. You miss the rope and you hit the ground.' Those were my instructions, and that was the end of my fast-roping career."

I was still looking out the window, watching the antiterrorist forces deploy. Visibility was practically nil on the mountainside under the helicopters because the wash of the rotors was kicking the snow off the ground and nearby trees. I could only see an occasional movement within the rotor wash, but I knew well enough that the soldiers would be fanning out in a circle as they hit the ground, each covering an arc to maintain 360-degree coverage for the protection of the team. After the team was on the ground, the helo lifted and the team leader cupped his hands over his ear to listen to his earpiece. The team formed up and moved slowly along the hillside toward the tree line, keeping their fields of fire covered. The same drill was going on in five other places as the Blackhawks delivered their people. Some were put down on the mountain and some closer to the city. Hunt was going to have his hands full if they found him.

"Can you find us a better view of the hill?" LeJeune asked the driver. With a nod, the driver took us to higher ground just east of town. From our vantage point there, we could see another stick of soldiers working its way toward higher ground on another ridge.

I didn't know who authorized their deployment, but I did know the Fed's antiterrorist team didn't come out to play unless things were very serious. They would be staged in Salt Lake throughout the Games, just in case, but they wouldn't be here on the hill unless this incident was being taken very seriously. LeJeune apparently had some influence somewhere. I supposed that the detonation of explosive devices, first at an international airport and then so close to an Olympic venue, was plenty of cause to get the big boys off the bench and into the game. What little I did know about these guys told me they were aching for a chance to work like a bull waits for the gates to swing open at a rodeo.

For me, the wait was agonizing. LeJeune was apparently in contact with the command center and was able to get updates on the status of the search.

"Not much to report," he said to me after one of his radio transmissions.

The whole situation was starting to seem familiar. We thought we'd had Hunt cornered at the oil refinery. That incident ended in the death of my best friend and Hunt's "miraculous" escape.

"He's not on the mountain." I turned to LeJeune, and said matter-of-factly. "He's in the city."

"What?" LeJeune asked.

"Look in the city," I repeated.

"What makes you so sure?"

"Where would you run?"

LeJeune gave a new set of orders on the radio, and our driver turned the Suburban around and started down the hill toward the city.

We had just turned into the historical district along Main Street when I saw Hunt walking quickly down the sidewalk, checking over his shoulder.

"Stop!" I shouted to the driver. The tires chirped and we came to an abrupt stop that threw me forward in my seat. Ignoring a stab of pain, I flung open the door and lunged out into the street. Hunt turned to see what the noise was, and we locked eyes. I tried to yell his name, but I didn't have the breath, gasping over the searing of my bullet wound. I took a few labored steps forward, willing myself to run after him, but Hunt was not as severely injured as I was, and he darted into the crowed before either LeJeune or I could catch him. Hunt had escaped again.

LeJeune forged into the swelling crowd of tourists to follow Hunt, but seeing me collapse in the street, he hesitated and then ran back to me.

On my knees, I held my side and fought back a wave of nausea. There was a considerable amount of fresh blood on the pavement, and LeJeune, realizing now how badly I was injured, ordered an ambulance by radio.

"We can't lose him again," I said. "You have to go after him."

"He can't get out of this town," LeJeune reassured me. "This place is locked down like Alcatraz."

I noticed a small commotion in the crowd and saw people turning their heads to look up the street. LeJeune noticed too and stood up to get a better view. I could tell by the reaction of the crowd something significant was happening.

"What's going on up there?" LeJeune screamed into his radio, standing on his tiptoes. "What's going on?"

"Why did I ever doubt?" I croaked.

"What?" LeJeune looked down at me.

We both looked back into the crowd and saw what had caused the stir.

Cutting a path through the crowd was Al, and he was walking an injured and bleeding Raymond Hunt along the sidewalk. Hunt was restrained by one of Al's famous sticky-ickky wristlocks, his left elbow pointed straight up. Al was casually walking along with a good grip on Hunt's wrist and fingers. Every time Hunt tried to resist, Al would simply twist his hand and Hunt would grimace.

LeJeune screamed orders in his radio and instructed the driver to block the road. When Al saw the dark Suburban, and me kneeling in the street, he was visibly relieved. He smiled and lifted four in the air—code four with one in custody.

Al gracefully changed the angle of his grip on Hunt's arm and drove Hunt slowly to his knees. Four FBI operators, their MP5 machine guns hanging in front of them on team slings, surrounded Hunt and gave him curt commands to get on the ground. Al released his grip, and Hunt was taken into custody by four of the world's most capable soldiers. The leader of the antiterrorist group, a powerfully built, middle-aged man with his blond hair cut in an immaculate flattop, turned his piercing blue eyes toward LeJeune and gave him a confident nod.

Raymond Hunt was toast.

EPILOGUE

Shortly after the excitement abated, it was to the hospital for me. The Park City Police Department had gotten a frantic call from Julianna with a wild story about mayhem in the mines, but by that time, the cavalry was already charging through the mountains searching for Hunt. Julianna had been taken to Snow Creek Emergency Center for treatment and had heard only snippets of what was going on. Her injuries were relatively minor—a broken ankle and some abrasions.

My injuries were a little uglier. I had twenty-seven stitches along my jawbone where a piece of the mine had torn the side of my face off. The doctor assured me he'd fashion the scar to be ruggedly handsome. Aside frm the burns on my hands and face, the most serious of my many injuries was a puncture in my back that had torn my left lung slightly, and of course, the bullet wound in my side that had done relatively minor damage.

Later in the day, LeJeune came with his family to visit me. His wife was pretty enough to stop traffic on Interstate 15, and his three kids were the ugliest, New Yorkiest boys I'd ever seen. They looked like Lem.

During his visit, LeJeune crowed about how I owed the federal government for biohazardous clean-up in his precious Suburban. Evidently the driver wasn't thrilled with my blood all over everything. LeJeune handed me a bill for $987.68 on a napkin and told me, "Hey, this is the way it's done in New York. You make the check out to the LeJeune family education fund." Then he let out a big New York guffaw. "Actually, the Feds are picking up the tab, including a new transmission for a Plymouth Roadrunner."

"I can explain," I said.

"I don't even want to know." LeJeune waved his hand. "Jimmy Rockford, for heaven's sake," he said under his breath.

Amanda and Julianna protected me from the throngs of reporters that had descended on the hospital to salvage what had been a slow news day up until then. As was normal, the media picked up on only the most obvious details of the incident, and professional government media types were spinning the rest of the story into oblivion. A few of the Fed soldiers had been in to see me briefly before being whisked away into obscurity to await another international disaster.

That evening, the only people left in my hospital room were Julianna, the LeJeune clan, Al, and Amanda. Al was trying to make it sound as though he almost accidentally ran into Hunt on the sidewalk. LeJeune and I knew better. Al had a way of being right where you needed him.

"Oh, I almost forgot to tell you, Owen," said Al.

"What?"

"The department is going to put you back on full duty as a detective, except . . ."

"Except what?"

"Except, when you go back to work, you'll be on light duty until you're fully healed."

"Ironically, it's okay this time," I said.

"And why is that?" asked Amanda.

"Well, that's simple. Now, when a pretty girl comes to the front desk and asks why I'm not out on patrol catching bad guys, I don't have to tell her I'm borderline insane. I can tell her that I was gravely injured saving the Olympics from a homicidal maniac. It just goes over so much better."

Everyone had a good laugh except Julianna, who was giving me a well-deserved glare.

"Hey guys," said LeJeune. "I've been waiting until all the riffraff left to show you this." He hefted the aged wooden box up onto my bed and plopped it down. The jarring hurt, and I groaned slightly.

LeJeune made a face. "What are you? A big wimp?"

"Is that it?" I'd only seen the box briefly in daylight. It looked older and more rustic now that I had a chance to examine it.

LeJeune was trying to hide the fact that he was starting to mist up, and so was his beautiful, blond wife. "I opened it about an hour ago," said LeJeune. "I didn't know what it was." He snorted again and wiped his nose on his sleeve. His wife gave him a sweet look and shook her head.

"I don't know how you did it." He pulled open the corroded box to reveal a sheaf of yellowed papers, tipping the box so I could see. The heading on the first page read, *The Journals of Rebecca Burns.*

"What are they?" asked Al. He and Amanda were straining to see.

"These, my friends, are my family journals." LeJeune was openly crying now and making horrible grunting noises.

"Your birth family?" Al asked.

LeJeune nodded. "This isn't all." He gently lifted the top several sheets of paper up to expose a charcoal drawing of a man standing amongst a tent city.

"What do you make of that, Owen? Where do you get off being in my family pictures? This guy here," he held a picture up in front of me, "he's the spitting image of you."

LeJeune was just joking, but what he didn't know was that the picture actually was of me. It was just one more bit of proof that I wasn't destined for the loony bin. In a rare moment of seriousness, he shook my hand and told me he was glad I was alive. Then he became his boisterous self again and started to herd his family out of the room.

"I guess that's our cue, Al," said Amanda. "Let's let these two have a little privacy."

"Privacy? What for?" asked Al.

"I'll explain it all to you later, dear," Amanda said. She dragged Al toward the door and halfway across the room before he turned around.

"Here," he said, pulling a brown paper bag from inside his coat. "Just in case you need a little pick-me-up." He pulled a four pack of Hostess Cupcakes from the bag and threw them on my lap. I could hear him laughing all the way down the hall. What a card.

"What was that all about?" asked Julianna when they left.

"Don't tell anybody, but Al really loves Hostess cuisine," I whispered. "Someone should warn Amanda before it's too late."

"Oh, by the way, it's too late. He proposed this morning. That's why you couldn't find him after he got off work."

"Figures. I hope she can stand him. He's an Oakland A's fan, you know."

"Oh, is that bad?"

"Oh, Ju," I moaned.

Julianna shook her head and smiled.

"I'm sorry, Ju. I really am. I never meant for all this to involve you."

"I know that," she said, caressing a part of my face not covered with bandages.

There was a knock at the open door, and then a head popped around the curtain into the room.

"May we?" Before I had a chance to say anything, Elder Rose and Elder Cannon barged in.

"Hi guys," I said. "I should probably introduce you to Julianna."

"Uh, hi," said Julianna. She was looking back and forth from me to the elders, obviously trying to put things together.

"Julianna," I said, pointing to the two men who were now standing by my bedside, "This is Elder Rose. The guy behind him is Elder Cannon."

Both men shook her hand. "We've been working on this guy," said Elder Rose. "We had to get special permission to come visit. We promised the mission president it would be worth it. Has he told you the—"

"No!" I yelled, then gained a little composure. "No, not yet. I just couldn't find the right time."

"Time for what? Tell me what?" asked Julianna, more than curious now.

"Well, it's more of a request," I said.

"Oh, really?"

"Yeah. Will you . . . will you . . ."

Julianna had turned to stone.

"Will you sing—at my baptism?"

"Sing? At your . . ." Julianna didn't say another word, but buried her face in my chest and cried.

"You know, this means you don't have a good excuse not to date me. You're going to have to fish for another one."

"You are such a doofus." She peeked up at me.

"I love you," I blurted, unable to control myself even in front of the elders.

"I love you too, Owen. I don't think I'll be needing that excuse. And yes, I'll sing at your baptism. How about *Unforgettable*?"

"At my baptism? Oh, funny," I said.

"When did all this happen?" she asked.

Elder Rose spoke up. "We've been teaching Owen for about two months now. We're all ready except for deciding on a baptism date."

"Oh, the date," I said. "Elder Rose, would you hand me my jacket? It's in the bag in the closet."

Elder Rose carefully pulled the tattered, bloody jacket from the bag and held it out to me on the end of his finger. I took it and pulled an index card from the inside breast pocket. It would be the second time these elders had seen Sister Kennedy's Message From Home.

"Anyone have a pen?" I asked. Two pens were shoved my way at lightning speed. I scribbled the date on the back of the card and showed it to Julianna.

"What's that?" asked Julianna.

"This is the date of my baptism. I hope you can make it."

"I wouldn't miss it." She was crying again.

I turned the card over and, for the first time since receiving it, I read the scripture to myself. *For verily I say unto you, If ye have faith as a grain of a mustard seed, ye shall say unto this mountain, Remove hence to yonder place; and it shall remove; and nothing shall be impossible unto you.*

It was my turn to mist up.

"May I?" Julianna asked gently after I'd had a moment to collect myself.

"Here," I whispered to her. "It's just a little Message From Home."

Julianna read the scripture and wrapped her arms around me.

The elders apparently realized their company was a bit awkward. "So, we should be going now," said Elder Rose. "We'll look you up in a few days and hash out the logistics of your baptism. You know, the date and everything."

We were only half listening to Elder Rose. Elder Cannon had his hand on Elder Rose's shoulder as they walked toward the door, likely congratulating themselves for a job well done. After they were gone, neither Julianna nor I moved. We were just content to soak up the moment.

The privacy curtain opened again, and a nurse entered the room. "Just checking on you, Owen. How are you feeling?" She was holding my yellow and blue Mariner's hat.

"Hey! I've been looking for that." I reached for the hat. "Where did you find it?"

"The two guys who've been holding up the wall outside your room hung it on the door latch as they were leaving."

"What two guys? The missionaries?"

"Nope. These guys didn't look like missionaries. One was a tall, good-looking young man with the most gorgeous green eyes I've ever seen, and the other was an older, distinguished-looking gentleman with a silver mustache, a long black trench coat, and a dark fedora."

Julianna gave me a puzzled look.

"I'll explain later," I said, grinning.

"Give a buzz if you need me." The nurse smiled and then disappeared behind the curtain.

Julianna gingerly stretched her arms around my broken body as best she could and rested her head on my good shoulder. I pulled the hat onto my head and Julianna into my arms.

"It's a perfect fit."

"Your hat?" Julianna asked, smiling up at me.

"No. You in my arms," I said, and then I kissed her.

All was well with the world. Now, if only I could convince this girl to marry me . . .

About the Author

Willard (Bill) Gardner is a police officer with the Pullman, Washington Police Department, where he serves as a detective, Youth Services/D.A.R.E. Officer, and a member of the SWAT team. He graduated from Washington State University (the other Cougars) with a master's degree in English and teaching credentials.

Bill enjoys reading, writing, playing the piano and guitar, working out, and most of all, spending time with his family. With four older sisters, a wife, two daughters, and two dogs of the genteel gender, Bill cheerfully admits to being outnumbered by his girls and has become quite proficient at vacuuming, washing dishes, shopping for outfits (accessories included), and buying roses.

Bill loves the Seattle Mariners, old movies, and staying home. *Pursuit of Justice* is the sequel to Bill's first novel, *Race Against Time.*

Bill enjoys corresponding with his readers, who can write to him in care of Covenant Communications, P.O. Box 415, American Fork, Utah 84003-0416, or e-mail him via Covenant at info@covenant-lds.com.